D0502277

Witch Dreams

Witch Dreams

Vivian Vande Velde

Marshall Cavendish

Marshall Cavendish Corporation
99 White Plains Road
Tarrytown, NY 10591
www.marshallcavendish.us

Library of Congress Cataloging-in-Publication Data
Vande Velde, Vivian.
Witch dreams / by Vivian Vande Velde.
p. cm.
Summary: Sixteen-year-old Nyssa uses her ability to see into people's dreams to discover who murdered her parents six years ago.
ISBN 0-7614-5235-4
[1. Dreams—Fiction. 2. Witches—Fiction. 3. Murder—Fiction.] I. Title.
PZ7.V2773Whr 2005
[Fic]—dc22
2004027571

The text of this set book is set in Cochin.
Book design by Anahid Hamparian

Printed in the United States of America
First edition
10 9 8 7 6 5 4 3 2

mc Marshall Cavendish

To Mary and Toni,

who continue to let me bounce ideas off them

—V. V. V.

One

Nyssa could dream other people's dreams.

By taking a token from someone.—a lock of hair, an article of clothing, something the person had touched or owned—and by placing this something beneath her pillow, Nyssa could share that person's dream.

Such bespelling never revealed ordinary dreams: no random wanderings of a sleeping mind in which past events and future possibilities tangled with never-could-be's. When Nyssa used her magic, the bespelled person might dream of his or her deepest desires or most heart-felt fears—and never suspect that those same dreams were simultaneously being experienced by Nyssa. Wish dreams felt cool and rippled, and fear dreams tasted rancid but were exciting. Nyssa thought herself most lucky when she saw a dream through the absolute clarity that signified true memory, for those dreams were the most interesting of all. True-memory dreams were more accurate than actual memories. They hid beyond ordinary dreams, beyond wish dreams or fear dreams, beyond the defenses formed by the lies people told others and by those they told themselves.

Still, Nyssa had learned from a young age that it was dangerous to practice witchcraft, and she never cast spells lightly or out of simple curiosity.

Yet one September night, while most of the citizens of the town of Lindenwolde slept, Nyssa felt the tingle of magic and knew a bespelled dream was about to begin. Having placed no token beneath her pillow, she realized her own arm had found its way there and had triggered the spell on herself. She was awake enough to want to pull her arm free, which would dislodge the dream, but she wasn't awake enough for her body to cooperate.

As she drifted deeper into sleep, she summoned enough energy to hope she was about to dream a wish dream. Or even a fear dream.

But the details were too clear. And whenever Nyssa dreamed her own true memories, she always saw the same event. The last six years disappeared. . . .

In the dream, Nyssa is once again ten years old. Though the sun is setting, spreading pink in the sky and shadows on the Earth, she is in the backyard of her parents' house. Her father is a woodworker, so they live on Woodworkers' Street. But as he is not very successful, they live at the south end, farther from the town square and well within the range of smells from Tanners' Alley, with its carcasses and its hides hung out to cure.

The more prosperous a customer is, she has heard her

father complain often enough, the more sensitive his nose is likely to be. Those who make it this far down the street, her father says, have thin purses and low expectations. He asks, "How can a woodworker who is talented but unlucky ever improve his situation?"

At this particular moment, Nyssa is not sympathetic to her father's situation. At this particular moment, she considers his complaints to be whining and his ill temper to be the reason that discerning customers avoid him.

Nyssa has hung one of the family's tapestries over the clothesline—the tapestry with the seafaring ships whose usual place is on the north wall of her father's shop. Though it is her mother's own handiwork, and Nyssa loves her mother, Nyssa hates the tapestry because the light blues and greens of sky and water show every bit of dirt. She has to beat this one twice as often and twice as hard as any other to keep it clean.

But, as the evening sheds its last light over Lindenwolde, she isn't beating loose the dust. She is sitting on the ground, exhausted from her earlier frenzied attack on the rug—not a cleaning attack, but a releasing of anger. Her left cheek no longer shows the imprint of her father's hand, but her ears still sting with his accusation of "Witch!"

Her brother, Worrell, sixteen years old and kind—when he takes the time to think about it—is crouched beside her, trying to tickle her neck with a blade of grass in order to get her to smile. "You just have to learn not to say things that upset him," Worrell tells her. Then he assures her, "He won't really send you away. Mother wouldn't allow it. I wouldn't allow it."

"I will watch my tongue, I promise," Nyssa says. Her father has always said she's a witless fool, and she knows he

must be right for she gets distracted and blurts out things she's learned from the dreams that have been visiting her in the two months since she turned ten. But Nyssa has enough wit to know a man has every right to ignore his wife's wishes—and his son's, and his daughter's—if he wants to send that daughter off to become a cloistered nun in a convent two weeks' journey away.

"I'll talk to him," Worrell promises.

Nyssa knows that will do no good, since Worrell himself isn't on the best of terms with Father.

Inside the house, Mother screams.

If this were a regular dream as regular folk dreamed, sixteen-year-old Nyssa, in her state of awake enough to be aware, could change it. She might make her mother come running out of the house screaming in fury because a frog had invaded her larder or because Father had somehow accidentally startled her.

Or if this were a regular memory as regular folk remembered, Nyssa could have convinced herself over the last six years that there had been no time for her to react, that there was nothing she could have done to change what was about to happen.

But this was a true-memory dream: unrelenting in its accuracy. No amount of wishing or trying to forget could change any part of it.

"Stay here," Worrell commands, his eyes wide, his face gone pale.

And only then does it occur to Nyssa that a good daughter would be desperate to rush into the house to see what has happened. Selfish, greedy, heedless—just as her father has always described her—she is thinking only of herself. She is too afraid to go into the house.

As she watches her brother race indoors, she tells herself, "Worrell said to stay." And, "I'd only get in the way."

So Nyssa stays.

"Father is in there," she tells herself after a while, "and now Worrell, too." Surely the two of them together can handle any situation.

Then why hasn't either of them come out—or Mother?

Dusk settles more firmly about the house and the yard.

The fear continues to grow in her belly. So does resentment. Haven't any of the neighbors heard? Shouldn't one of the other woodworkers come running to see what help is needed? Yet no one is astir. All Nyssa can hear is their neighbor's dog barking, incessantly, which is not a sign of anything, for Rufus barks all the time.

Nyssa considers getting up, beating the tapestry some more, or at least taking it down from the line. She thinks that if she can go about her ordinary routine, this will force an ordinary explanation of that scream and the subsequent long, long silence.

By now the yard is almost completely in shadow, and the silence has gone on for much too long. Soon the house will be totally darkened, for no candles have been lit inside, despite the fast-approaching night. Nyssa could go next door and ask for help from Thurmond or his apprentice, George, but she would rather cling this little bit longer to the belief that nothing is seriously wrong.

Nyssa forces herself to stand. Her legs are wobbly, and she tells herself that this is from sitting on the hard ground for so long. She approaches the door that Worrell has left open and concentrates on breathing through her nose, not her mouth. She must be quiet so that she can hear—she tells herself—her family laughing about whatever silly thing startled Mother.

There is no laughter.

She peeks in, afraid of what she'll see. She sees only the kitchen, in which her mother has not begun to prepare the evening meal.

In a small and shaky voice, she calls, "Worrell?" hoping that he will come to her.

But there is no answer.

She moves through the kitchen, down the hallway that is meant to protect the house from the heat of cooking in the summer, and then, finally, she sees Worrell. He is sitting in the doorway that leads from the living quarters to the woodworking shop, his back toward her. In the dim light she can barely make him out.

"Worrell?" she whispers.

He doesn't answer, but he brings his hand up to his face, and only then does Nyssa admit to herself that she had feared he was dead, that he was only propped up by the door frame.

"Worrell?" she repeats.

He stands and turns.

She wonders if it's really him, if she's mistaken an intruder for her brother, because he looks so big in the shadows of the unlit house as he moves toward her.

But close up she can recognize his face, and as he leans

down from his height to put his arms around her she smells on his hair the soap Mother makes, the soap to which Mother adds a drop of vanilla for its fresh scent despite Father faulting her extravagance. But in the moment before Worrell embraces her, Nyssa has seen something else, and she smells something else, and he's sobbing, though she's never before heard him cry. "Don't look in there," he warns her, so of course she looks over his shoulder, and despite the shadows, she sees two forms on the floor which she knows—though she tries not to know it—are her parents.

Not quickly enough, he turns her around, to face her away from the horror in that room.

"We have to help them," she says, finally thinking of them first, finally putting them before her—worthless, selfish thing that she is.

"Nyssa," he says, then more insistently, "Nyssa."

"They're hurt," she says, inanely, for surely he's seen that for himself in all the time he's been sitting here in the dark.

His fingers are digging into her arms to prevent her, now—now that it's too late—from rushing to their parents' aid.

"Nyssa." He gives her a little shake. He speaks the words out loud: "They're dead."

Now that he is standing straight, she can see the smear of darkness over his brow, and she's unable to convince herself this is just a shadow. She knows that what she's been smelling is his blood, that he has been injured.

Her parents have been murdered, and their murderer must have still been here when Worrell went in. Only her own cowardly delay kept her safe. This thought brings guilt rather than relief.

"You saw him?" she asks. Who could do such a thing? Her father doesn't have enough money for someone to kill him for it.

"Who?" Worrell asks.

"The man, or men, who did this?"

He shakes his head, then winces at the movement.

"You must have seen," she insists. "They hurt you, too."

His hand goes to the side of his head. He studies the blood on his fingers.

"Who was it?" she demands.

He's sounding vague, confused. "I . . . don't know."

"You must have seen," she repeats, for the wound is on his forehead. "At least a glimpse."

"Nyssa," he starts to say, then he sways, clutching the door frame to keep from falling.

"Hold on," she commands, meaning more than just to the door. Surely the wound isn't serious enough to . . . The most she'll permit herself to worry about is danger. Surely the wound isn't serious enough to endanger him. "I'll get help," she offers: anything—anything—to keep from having to go into that room. "You try to remember what you saw."

"Remember," Worrell echoes groggily. He sits down heavily on the floor, and Nyssa has to step over him to get past.

"I'll be right back," she reassures him.

"Back," Worrell repeats, scaring her more than if he had said nothing.

She runs down the hall, through the kitchen—smacking her shin against one of the chairs that's little more than a shadow in the evening's dimness. Now she's out in the backyard, running across it to their nearest neighbors.

And all the while she's running, she's remembering her father's words from when he slapped her earlier that afternoon. She starts screaming for help, to be heard above neighbor Thurmond's barking dog, to get people there faster, but also to drown out the memory of her father's voice which seems to chase her: "Witch. I'll send you away. By God, I'll send you to that abbey up by Sterling."

Surely she isn't the cause of what has happened, she tells herself. She has the power to bespell other people's dreams, to spy, to eavesdrop. Never before has she seen any sign that she has the power to make wishes come true.

And even if she did, she never really meant it when she wished her father dead.

And she never wished her mother ill.

Nor her brother.

But as the neighbors begin to stick their heads out of doors and windows to see what all the fuss is about, Nyssa can't stop the thought: "Father won't be sending me anywhere now."

Two

Nyssa jerked herself awake. She had been so caught up in the dream that she awoke confused. But one thing was clear: this wasn't her own room, her own bed. . . .

For one awful moment, she realized someone was lying next to her, and she couldn't think who that could be.

She recognized the surly grumble: "Lie still, girl. Just 'cause you can't sleep is no reason to wake everybody else up."

Peldrida, Nyssa realized with something like relief.

Her waking life resettled gently about her. Reality once more took shape. Nyssa no longer had her own bed in her own room in her own father's house. She shared a bed with the two other female servants in the household of Darton, the wool merchant, and his wife, Kermillie. While she was no longer in danger of being sent off against her will to a convent, neither would she be marrying some tradesman—even one who lived at the farthest end quickly and decisively, Nyssa restrained her fidgeting so as not to wake Aldo. Had it been Master Finn rather than Aldo in charge of the night fire, she would have poked at it until she'd disturbed him, for Master Finn was a spoiled brat. And for thirteen years old, he seemed unnaturally preoccupied with catching a glimpse of the servant women getting dressed or undressed. But she had no complaint with Aldo. She would do better to start getting water from the well three streets away before the other households' servants formed a line. Placing the buckets on the pole and the pole on her shoulders, she took off at a pace that was almost a half run and that would have been unseemly for a oung woman, if there had been anyone awake to otice.

Such mindless work did not disperse her oughts. If she were a clever girl, she could have used on some thorny question of politics or gion or economy rather than dwelling on her problems like—her father used to say—a dog ying a fleabite till it bled.

he went to the well and back twice. Then, just e began her third circuit, Nyssa heard the h bell ring. Soon there would be a cluster of but talkative under-servants at the well. a talkative girl herself, Nyssa veered off, the buckets swinging wildly at the ends of the still had balanced on her shoulders.

found herself, as she often did, in front of r house of Lord Haraford. The servants

of his trade's street. Nyssa had not expected to do better than her mother, had never envisioned having servants to tend her. But now she herself was a servant in another woman's household.

Being the youngest, Nyssa had to sleep in the middle, subject to both Peldrida, a restless sleeper who was all flailing elbows and bony knees—a fine one to be finding fault with one startled twitch—and Maddy, who slept with her mouth open, breathing her dank breath onto Nyssa.

There she was again, Nyssa thought, concerned only with herself, when she had just re-lived her parents' death.

And when the guilty man—the man she *knew* was guilty—was still free.

"Lie still!" Peldrida demanded a second time.

Nyssa had to fight the inclination to be moving, to be doing *something*. Not that there was anything to do, not that there had ever been anything to do—not after her own selfishness, her own worthlessness, had killed her parents. Over the past six years, Father William had tried to convince her that resenting your father, even hating your father—even wishing your father dead—would not kill him. "How could a wish," he asked, "an unspoken wish, influence someone to break into your parents' home?"

Someone. His name was Elsdon. Everyone knew his name was Elsdon. But only Nyssa was willing to say so.

Father William could have said: "How could a

wish influence Elsdon to break into your parents' home?" But Father William wouldn't blame Elsdon, whose parents had falsely sworn he was with them, and Father William didn't know she was a witch. He didn't know she had powers not covered in his catechism.

Maybe he was right and maybe he wasn't, about the power of her ill wishing. But Nyssa knew she was doubly responsible. For even if her thoughts hadn't caused the decision, she had still aided Elsdon. If she had run in immediately upon hearing her mother's scream, as any dutiful daughter would have, she could have helped her family overpower him.

Or, even if her parents had been already dead by the time she and her brother had burst into the room together, she could have prevented Worrell from being hurt.

At the very least she could have identified Elsdon, since Worrell's injury had left him too dazed to remember anything. The magistrates of Lindenwolde had not been willing to take the word of neighbor Thurmond, who had seen Elsdon fleeing from the house, nor of the other neighbors who testified to Elsdon's loitering in the neighborhood in the two or three days beforehand. He had commissioned a box to be fashioned, Elsdon claimed, and the work had been unsatisfactory—that was the business that had caused him to return several times to the shop. The magistrates were unimpressed when neighbors told them that Elsdon had

quarreled with her father that very afternoor
They didn't believe because they didn't *want*
believe. Elsdon's family's money bought their g
reputation.

But people would not have been able to i
Nyssa if she had been able to say, "I was t
saw."

If, if, if . . .

How could Nyssa lie still in the female
bed when her dreams and her thoughts
her?

Soon Peldrida's scolding would
Better to get up now, Nyssa thought,
feeling fully awake, than to stay in
the other women and then falling a
it would be time to get up for the

Peldrida and Maddy both
crawled out of bed and fetch
where it hung on a nail in the
the dark, then opened the door
a room and stepped out into
in the house was snoring
Mistress Kermillie in the m
son Finn in the room acro
the kitchen, Darton's ap
on his pallet by the hear

Quietly Nyssa ease
The sky was light gra
the east, and the chu
the day started, so t

Still fighting

were probably up already, though the lord and his lady most probably were not. Nyssa began singing—loudly, a bawdy song about the unlikely adventures of a randy stableboy who pursued, wooed, and won a lady whose husband remained oblivious to it all, through seven escalating verses. Not that Nyssa had any reason to believe anything of the sort was going on in the manor. Surely Lady Eleanor, who was *old*—who was *at least* forty—was too old to excite that sort of interest in a stableboy, or anyone else for that matter.

If the house had been closer to the street, Nyssa might have flung a rock or a clump of dirt at the master bedroom. But she'd have to enter the gate to be within throwing range, and the lord's servants had caught her often enough in the past. The risk was not worth the excitement, she decided.

Someone opened a window and yelled at her to shut up so early in the morning, and that was almost enough to encourage her to start the song all over again. Still, she needed to get back before Mistress Kermillie noticed her absence.

Nyssa ended her song, and in the quiet of the early morning heard hoofbeats on the dirt road behind her. She turned and saw two young men who—judging by their fine clothes and fine horses—were obviously bound for the manor. As they got closer, she recognized one of them as Ralf, and she discounted him as just a dressed-up servant from the house.

"Who's the songbird?" she heard the other ask.

He tossed a coin in her direction, which landed in the dirt at her feet.

As though she were a beggar. As though she'd been singing for their *entertainment,* rather than to annoy the lord and lady.

"Just crazy Nyssa," Ralf said. "She's mostly harmless."

"She still alive?" the other asked mildly.

Her father had called her witless because she didn't stop to think things out. Since that awful day, she had heard people suggest that her wits had suffered, citing the way she had hounded the magistrates for their decision, and the way she kept after Lord Haraford and his household, and the way—without her parents to look after her—she sometimes forgot to look after herself. Still, it stung to be dismissed as crazy, mostly harmless Nyssa.

But at least the riders had made no attempt to force her off the road or into the swan pond.

It wasn't until the men had passed that Nyssa recognized the second: Lord Haraford and Lady Eleanor's youngest son, who had been away for the past six years. The last time Nyssa had seen him, he had been fifteen years old, younger than she was now. She would have thought that he'd filled in nicely in those six years and gone from gawky to handsome, except for the look of disdain on his face.

That, and the fact that he was Elsdon, the man who had murdered her parents.

She let the buckets drop from her shoulders.

What was she going to do? Run after him and attempt to drag him off his horse? She had no plan in mind, but she was already moving when someone grabbed her from behind. "Nyssa."

"Let go of me!" Nyssa struggled against the restraining arms, and twisted, jabbing backward with her elbows.

Elsdon glanced over his shoulder to see what the disturbance was, but wasn't interested enough to stop. The horses kept moving, through the gate, into the manor yard. Despite the early hour, servants came out to tend to the young lord and his horse, and he never looked back again.

"*Nyssa.*" It was Worrell shaking her by the shoulders.

When he saw that he'd captured her attention, he let go and leaned over, his hands on his knees to catch his breath. He had on his guard's livery, as though he'd been on duty at the gate when Elsdon had entered the town, as though he had run all this way, dodging down alleys and over fences to get here before Elsdon. And not for any reason Nyssa could understand: not to drag the smug, little murderer off his horse and plunge a dagger into his heart. But to protect him. To protect him from Nyssa.

"I'll never understand you," she told Worrell from between clenched teeth. Even if she suddenly got as smart as her father—who had been smart enough to get people to pay more than they wanted, who had never been at a loss for words—she would never understand. Worrell still bore the scar on his forehead, red and indented, from the night he'd been unsuccessful in stopping Elsdon from killing their parents.

"Even," Worrell said, still panting from his run, "even if you were able to kill him, you would be sentenced to die."

"It would be worth it," Nyssa said.

Worrell ignored that comment. "But more likely, he or Ralf would just have run you down with their horses. Then you'd be dead and he wouldn't. Or if you weren't dead, you'd be crippled. You'd become a beggar living on the street because Kermillie wouldn't keep you on if you couldn't work. And no salary in the world would be enough to keep you supplied with medicines." Beyond that he added, "Which *still* wouldn't be enough to dull the constant pain."

"Dead, crippled, in pain, *and* out of work?" Nyssa demanded. "Don't you think you're being a little excessive in your gloom?"

"Of course I am," Worrell admitted. "I'm trying to make a point here."

Nyssa snorted, but her frenzied compulsion to get at Elsdon had subsided to controllable hate. "He killed our parents." She shouldn't have had to say it to Worrell. But the blow to his head had destroyed his memory, so he had been unable to reveal his assailant's name. And the magistrates had chosen to believe the lord and lady rather than the woodworkers and housewives. Nyssa spat out,

"There are different rules for the rich."

"And that," Worrell finished, "is nothing new in the world. We have been through this, Nyssa. They could do you great harm."

Nyssa said, "If only I could look into your dreams. . . ." She had tried the night she had become an orphan. And later. Nothing worked as a token: not the little carved wren that had been one of the first objects Father had taught Worrell to craft from wood, and not the blanket that Mother had woven for him years before, and not the strand of his hair that she had guarded after finding it on his own pillow. Whatever he dreamed—if he dreamed—she could not see any more than she could see into the minds of her murdered parents—though Father William said they slept in Christ. "Maybe," Nyssa said, "I could try again."

"You know that wouldn't work," Worrell said. It was as close as he ever came to calling her witless.

"But—"

"Stop," Worrell commanded her.

And she knew he was right. It would do no good anyway. Even if she could see Elsdon in Worrell's true-memory dreams, either the magistrates would not believe in her power to re-create the murder scene, so that she would be branded as a perjurer, and Elsdon would go free; or the magistrates *would* believe in her power—and she would be condemned as a witch.

And, still, Elsdon would go free.

"It's not fair." Even as she said it, she knew that she sounded like a two-year-old, young enough to be surprised to find the world composed of sharp angles and hard surfaces. "If it weren't for him, our parents would still be alive, and you'd be a wood carver in your own right by now." She tugged at the shoulders of his ill-fitting uniform.

"With Father in charge?" Worrell gave a dismissive snort. "I'd be the world's oldest apprentice."

Father *had* been stubborn, always finding fault with others' ways of doing things.

But he wouldn't have given the shop to strangers.

And she . . .

You're being selfish again, she reminded herself. *Thinking about yourself and your problems. Again.*

Worrell shook her by the shoulders to get her attention. "Stop dwelling on it," he told her.

"I can't help it," she said. "It was hard enough while Elsdon was away. . . ."

"Leave him alone," Worrell said. "Leave Lord Haraford and Lady Eleanor alone. People have accepted your behavior because of how you lost your family. But you're no longer a child. They're going to lose patience with you."

Nyssa knew he was right. She nodded toward the manor yard, though Elsdon and all the servants had gone indoors. "Ralf called me crazy," she admitted.

Worrell tipped her face up so that she had to

look into his eyes. "Well," he told her, "everybody's a little crazy when they're sixteen."

"You weren't," she said.

He ignored her words. "Didn't you even comb your hair this morning?"

"I forgot again," she admitted. Nor had she bothered to wash her face. Now that she thought about it, she realized she hadn't even used the privy. Now that she thought about it, she really *should* have used the privy.

Worrell was shaking his head. "This must stop."

Reluctantly, she nodded.

He said, "And you probably have just enough time to get back before Kermillie notices you're away and you get in trouble."

Nyssa rolled her eyes but nodded.

"Take the shilling he threw."

"I don't need *his* charity."

"Of course not," Worrell agreed. "But no matter where it comes from, the money is enough to buy a ribbon for your hair, or to get your shoes mended if Kermillie gets into one of her stingy moods. There's no benefit in leaving money on the street just because it's Elsdon's."

Elsdon's.

Nyssa picked up the coin, not because she would use it to *buy* anything, but because she could use Elsdon's coin for something else, for something that would really benefit her. She kept her face bland lest Worrell read the thought in her mind and try to dissuade her.

"Go." Worrell was waiting to make sure she left.

She left.

Ribbon, she thought as she rushed through the streets. *Shoes.* She'd almost lost the chance to get something of Elsdon's into her possession. A token. In the past she had tried to sneak her way into the manor house to find something of his with which to bespell his dreams, but she'd always been caught and been run off—and the last time she'd been told if she did it again she would be punished. And now she had almost left this coin in the street. If she was going to prove that Elsdon had murdered her parents, she would have to start being smarter.

And maybe, she thought, proving that Elsdon had murdered her family would erase some of her own guilt.

Three

By the time Nyssa got back to the wool merchant's house, Mistress Kermillie was already awake and in the kitchen overseeing the setting out of the breakfast Peldrida and Maddy had prepared.

"And where have you been?" the mistress demanded with a sour scowl, as though she had been left abandoned to do the entire running of the world with her own hands.

"Getting water." Nyssa stopped by the hearth to take the pole off her shoulders. She kept her back to the wall, because the wretched young master, Finn, was already at the table. If she leaned over in his presence, he was sure to brush his hand against her rump, which his mother—who normally had very keen eyesight—never seemed to see. Nyssa set the buckets down carefully, hoping they wouldn't tip or rattle, hoping the mistress wouldn't realize they were empty.

But of course the mistress *did*. "Light load," she said with a sneer. "Surely even a witless, worthless girl like you should have noticed that you, in fact, forgot to bring the water home with you."

Witless, worthless girl. Nyssa wondered if, somehow, however distantly, this sharp-tongued woman could be related to her on her father's side.

"I already brought two loads back before the morning bell." Nyssa hurried to slice the bread and set it on the table, to make herself look useful. "But the third time I went, there was such a line, I thought it was better to return rather than wait." Nyssa knew she wasn't a good liar—she wasn't smart enough to be creative and believable—but she *was* good at leaving out details, and she hoped this would suffice.

Kermillie walked over to the water vat to check the level. "Hmph," she said, neither accusing Nyssa outright of lying, nor admitting her own mistake.

While his mother's back was turned, Finn took the opportunity to rest his hand against Nyssa's backside.

Nyssa stepped away and glared, which was all she dared do.

"Go!" Kermillie ordered Nyssa, waving her hand in dismissal. "None of us wants to look at your slovenly self while we're eating. Since you haven't cleaned yourself, I believe it's time the privy was cleaned."

That was how the day went. Throughout, Kermillie gave Nyssa one miserable task after another, perhaps peeved that nothing she ordered could dampen Nyssa's mood. That was because

Nyssa didn't care what she did to make the day pass—every chore she worked at, no matter how odious, brought her closer to the night.

And then night finally came, and Nyssa got into the bed she shared with the two other servants. Peldrida and Maddy chatted for a bit, but Nyssa didn't hear their words. She held Elsdon's coin clenched in her fist beneath the pillow and brought the features of Elsdon's face into her mind. Over and over she mentally repeated his name.

First Peldrida and Maddy tried to draw her into conversation; then, tired of talking back and forth over her prone body, they settled down for sleep.

Bespelling could easily go wrong since there was no way to control what kind of dream Nyssa would find herself looking into: wish, fear, or true memory. Once when Maddy had lost Mistress Kermillie's best sewing needle and the mistress had had the whole house in an uproar searching for it and still it had not shown up by evening, Nyssa had thought to use her magic to discover its whereabouts. She looked into Maddy's dreams, thinking to see where Maddy had absentmindedly set down the missing needle. Instead, when the bespelled dream began, Nyssa had found that she wasn't experiencing the sharp details of a true-memory dream but was feeling the cool, soft ripple effect of a wish dream. And the wish dream had concerned Maddy and a certain handsome, young potter's assistant who declared his undying love with hugging and kissing—and more—to a degree that should certainly have shamed a decent girl.

Now Nyssa fell asleep thinking of Elsdon. She hoped the coin would work even though, having passed through many people's hands, money was the least likely of a person's possessions to link her to that person's dreams. She also hoped that as Elsdon drifted off to sleep he would remember seeing her that morning, and that his sleeping mind would return to her and her family so that she could snag a true-memory dream of that evening six years before.

Nyssa felt herself slip quickly into Elsdon's sleeping mind. She was aware of herself long enough to realize that he had to have been asleep already. *Tired,* she deduced, for he must have traveled through the night in order to have come riding through the town gate first thing in the morning.

A guilty, soul-searing memory would be nice about now, she thought, a moment before she lost herself. But instead of seeing with the absolute clarity of a true-memory dream, Nyssa tasted the rancid taste of a fear dream.

Elsdon dreams that he has just awakened from a dream. He doesn't remember what he has just experienced, but his heart is racing and he has the feeling of having narrowly escaped.

Now he dreams that he lies in the dark and wonders where he is. Not a bed, for the surface beneath him is hard, and the darkness is too deep for his room.

He sits up, and absolutely nothing in the darkness shifts.

He tries to stand and smacks his head on a ceiling only a hand's span or so above where his head had been when he was sitting. Is this a tunnel? he wonders. He touches the ceiling, raps his knuckles against what sounds and feels like wood. He stretches his arms out to either side, and his fingertips just barely reach to touch walls, also of wood. Is he a prisoner? In some sort of wooden cage or trap?

He tries to think back to the last thing he can remember before going to sleep, to work out where he could be, or at least how he could have gotten here. Or who could have put him here.

But his life before waking up a few moments ago is a blank. If the dream that woke him had any clues, that, too, is gone.

He feels the ceiling pressing lightly on his head, and he wonders if he hit his head so hard that a huge bump is forming. But when he reaches up, his head feels fine. It's the ceiling that appears to have moved down.

Elsdon reaches out to the sides and realizes those walls have moved in also.

"Hey!" Elsdon yells, banging his fist on the ceiling.

The only response is that the ceiling moves down farther yet.

Elsdon can no longer remain sitting up.

He has to either duck forward or lean back on his elbows. He leans back. He once again yells, "Hey!" and bangs his heels on the surface beneath.

If there is anyone outside his quickly diminishing prison, that person is not making a sound.

The walls close in again. Elsdon, now flat on his back, braces his arms, elbows on the floor, palms up against the ceiling.

The ceiling moves down anyway, an inexorable force, so that his arms are now jammed into position. Elsdon knows he is not strong enough to prevent the ceiling from moving down again, and he knows that—if the ceiling moves lower—the bones in his forearms will shatter.

He manages to slide his palms sideways, which unwedges his arms. A moment later, the ceiling once again edges closer to his face.

Elsdon has his arms down by his sides, and he can feel the walls pressing them against his body. The ceiling is about a handbreadth away from his face. He can probably survive one more closing in. The one after that will crush his skull.

He is breathing too hard to be able to call out. Besides, he suspects that once he starts screaming, he will not be able to stop. He doubts that his screaming or not screaming will have any effect on those who control the box, and he hopes to maintain his dignity.

The walls do not move again.

Instead there's the sound of something striking the outside of his prison, a thud and a skitter, and Elsdon is just barely able to hold on to his resolve not to scream.

A voice says, matter-of-factly, "Of course he can't be buried in hallowed ground."

Followed by another thud and skitter.

Which Elsdon recognizes this time as a shovelful of dirt hitting the top and running down the sides of the coffin he's in.

"Hey!" he yells, and beats his feet up and down on the ceiling and floor.

Thud and skitter.

"Hey!" This time he keeps on yelling, keeps on kicking. Over the sounds of his noise, he can hear the thud and skitter of more shovelfuls of dirt.

"Stop!" His throat feels scratchy from the loudness of his shouts, and he pauses to regain his strength, to keep from crying.

A second voice asks, "You hear something?"

As Elsdon takes in a lungful of air, he hears the first voice say, "Nope," and there's another thud and skitter, muffled this time, since a layer of dirt already covers him.

"Stop!" Elsdon screams. "Stop, stop, stop!" But he can't hear the voices anymore, and after a while he can't hear the dirt, either.

Nyssa's heart was racing from the fear she had shared with Elsdon. She pictured him sitting up in bed, which she knew was pure imagination, because she didn't have the power to watch people, only to see their dreams. It should have been a pleasant little dream of her own, seeing him in a panic, stretching his arms out to make sure the walls were where they were supposed to be; that he was, in fact, in his own bed in his own room; that the dream wasn't starting all over again. But the terror they had both experienced through his dream had unsettled her.

It was a terrible dream, even for someone who deserved it.

It was almost enough to make her feel sorry for him. Almost. Except that she took the dream as proof of his guilt. He *was* thinking about how he had murdered her parents. But instead of getting a true-memory dream of the events as they'd happened, his dream had been formed by his fear of getting caught and punished.

She forced herself to lie back down, to lie still, her breathing calm. She clutched the coin in her sweaty palm. *Elsdon,* she thought. *Elsdon.* And pictured his face. And worked the magic to once again see his dreams.

She fell asleep with her mind open, and dreamed only her own vague, wandering, regular-dream images.

Morning arrived with the clanging of the Lindenwolde church bell, with no more dreams from Elsdon. Had the power of the coin faded?

No. Somehow she was sure of it. She pictured him sitting up in his bed all night, huddled in the dark with his knees drawn up to his chest, afraid to lie back down, afraid to go back to sleep, preferring sleeplessness to the chance of another nightmare.

That was all right, Nyssa thought. He'd fall asleep eventually.

Four

After the wool merchant's family had been served their breakfast, the servants ate. Then Nyssa cleaned up the kitchen and poked her head into the master bedroom. "Has the mistress gone to the market yet?" she asked. But she knew as soon as she asked—for she was just in time to see Maddy sweep a pile of dust under the rug while Peldrida dusted around the comb and mirror and pots of ointment on the mistress's nightstand rather than clear everything off to clean properly. They wouldn't have dared such sloppiness if Kermillie had still been in the house, for sometimes Kermillie snuck up on people precisely to catch them doing something they shouldn't be.

Peldrida told Nyssa, "Mistress has gotten it into her head that the baker puts out the best breads first and that he adds extra yeast in what he sells later in the morning, so she's determined to get the full weight she's due, even if she has to be at the bakery before full light."

Nyssa wasn't interested in how the mistress

planned to outsmart the merchants she was sure were cheating her. She said, "Unless you need me here, I'll fill up the water vat."

Peldrida gave her a long look, then shrugged and said, "As you choose."

A smarter girl could have come up with a more plausible justification to leave the house, but then probably a smarter girl wouldn't be working in Kermillie's household. Nyssa had believed fetching water to be a good excuse since—as the youngest servant in the household—this task most often fell to her anyway. Perhaps it was her volunteering that made Peldrida suspect her motives.

Still, Nyssa took up the water buckets, though she headed off in the direction opposite from the well, toward her former neighborhood.

She saw Elsdon, watching her.

Across the street and two doors down from Master Darton's establishment was a tavern where, weather permitting, Barlow the tavern keeper placed tables outside so customers could sit and watch the traffic on the street. Despite the early hour, despite the lack of company and the fact that surely there were finer taverns closer to his home, there Elsdon sat, elbow on table, chin on fist, staring directly at her.

This had to be a coincidence, Nyssa told herself, his sour expression evidence of general bad temper or from lack of sleep rather than from knowledge that she'd spied on him. People weren't aware of her looking into their dreams. Her family had known of her ability only because, at age ten when the power had first started and before she'd learned any better, she had told them. "I saw you holding Worrell when he was a baby and he was so sick you thought he was going to die, and you stood outside so the rain would cool his fever," she had told her mother, having seen something in a true-memory dream from a time before she'd been born, a time no one had told her about.

And to Worrell, "I saw you and Father working side by side in the shop, and he told you, 'Good work—I'm proud of you,' and he never yelled, not once"—obviously a wish dream and never a true memory.

And to her father, "I saw you making a chest that was so ornate and fine, the master of the Woodcrafters' Guild resigned and named you his successor and the Pope came and begged to buy it from you to keep Saint Peter's relics in," never knowing how angry her father would be to have his secret wish dream revealed.

"Yes," Mother had said, "I was just remembering that in my sleep last night."

"Yes," Worrell had said. "That's exactly what I dreamed."

"Don't ever let me hear of you doing such a thing again," her father had said, "you perverted, little abomination."

Nyssa had long ago realized it would have been better if she had been born not able to speak. A silent girl, who knew enough to stay out of Father's way.

Still, her trouble came from telling her family what she had seen in their dreams. They had not known until then.

So there was no way Elsdon could *really* have seen her watching him, despite her having had the sense of seeing him sitting up, sleepless, in his bed. That was just imagination on her part, when she couldn't capture any more of his dreams. He hadn't really seen her, any more than she had really seen him.

She looked over her shoulder as she walked, to make sure he wasn't following her—just as he caught hold of her arm.

Nyssa jerked back, but he didn't let go. "Stay away from my house," he hissed. "Stop plaguing me."

For one confused moment, she had to remind herself yet again that he couldn't be telling her to keep away from his dreams—for there was no way for him to know she had anything to do with them. He must be referring to seeing her the previous morning in front of his house. Couldn't he tell her presence there had been a coincidence? How could she have known he would have chosen that day, that moment, after these six years, to return?

But this made her wonder: why *had* he come back anyway? Was he arrogant enough to think that six years and his family's wealth could make people forget?

"I know what you are," she told him.

"I know what *you* are," he countered.

Which probably meant "too crazy for anyone to listen to" and "too poor to count for anything."

But it was still a frightening thing to hear him say.

Her father had beaten her for being a witch, and many would consider that unduly lenient. The law called for witches to be put to death.

Nyssa jerked her arm again, and this time Elsdon released her so that she and her buckets fell back against the wall of the bakery they were standing by. She said, "You leave me alone, and I'll leave you alone," meaning only: *no more early morning singing in front of your house.* Of course she would continue to try to have him proved guilty of murder.

He didn't respond, and she took that to mean agreement. She hoped. She backed away from him, and he made no move to stop her, even when she went around the corner.

After several steps, she glanced over her shoulder. No sign of him.

A few more steps, another look.

He was standing there at the corner, watching her.

But he made no move to follow farther.

She stumbled, from walking, then glancing, walking, then glancing.

By the time she was halfway down the street, he was gone from the corner, and she didn't see him anywhere.

Which was reassuring.

Except that she suddenly remembered what he'd said when Ralf had identified her in the street in front of the manor house. *She still alive?* she remembered Elsdon asking.

That had been before she'd peeked into his dreams, before he should have had any reason to be provoked by her.

Now she finally took the time to ask herself, *Now, what in the world would have made him ask that?*

It wasn't that her old home held happy memories, but it was disconcerting to see others living in the place where she had been born. Nyssa stood across the street, recognizing the neighbors' houses and businesses, seeing children running and playing whom she had only known as babies, so that she had to guess by family resemblance who they might be. Her childhood home looked shabbier than she remembered, which it could have gotten to be, but it also looked smaller, which couldn't have happened. The door to her father's old shop was open—most merchants had their doors open in good weather, to let in any breeze and to invite potential customers to examine their wares. Through the doorway she could see two woodcrafters assembling a chest. She had heard two families had moved in where previously there had been only hers. The new artisans had their stock displayed: chairs that struck her even from this distance as not being as well made as her father's; wooden boxes of different designs from those he had crafted; stools, small tables, bowls, combs, polished statues of saints.

She crossed the street beyond the house, so that she wouldn't have to walk directly in front of it, the way children sometimes cross the street to avoid walking too close to a cemetery. A dog came running up to her, barking, and she tensed, afraid it was going to bite. But it was wagging its tail; and once her fear subsided, Nyssa saw the creature was Rufus, the dog of Thurmond, their old neighbor.

Sadly, Thurmond didn't look as alert as his dog. He sat in a chair on the front stoop, so still he seemed part of the chair—like a life-sized but not exactly lifelike doorstop carved by a woodcrafter of grotesque genius. Propped upright with pillows, he was prevented from sliding off the chair by a leather strap that crisscrossed over his chest. Someone, probably one of his sisters, had placed a blanket on his lap and over his legs. This would have been a kindness first thing in the morning, but the day was getting warm enough that Thurmond probably would have kicked the blanket off if he'd had any ability to control his legs.

But of course if he could control his legs, he wouldn't have been strapped to his chair. All of this was a consequence of having fallen last summer while repairing the roof over the chapel in Lord Haraford's manor. Nyssa had come to visit him shortly after the accident, and he'd looked better then: in pain, and angry from it. Now his jaw was slack, his chin shiny with spittle, his eyes half closed as though he didn't have the energy or the will to look out into the world.

Over his shoulder, Nyssa could see into his shop, where a young man was smoothing a length of cherrywood with a plane, oblivious to her and to the old man in the chair. George, Nyssa guessed, Thurmond's nephew. He had changed so much, going from young apprentice to man, that Nyssa wouldn't have recognized him except for seeing him here. He looked to have aged at least a dozen years since she'd last seen him four or five years ago—as opposed to Worrell, who never got older to Nyssa's eyes. And as opposed to Elsdon, who had only improved with age.

Horrified to find herself having *any* kind thought about Elsdon, Nyssa approached the slack figure bound to the chair.

"Thurmond?" She would have thought that the barking of the dog would have let him know a visitor had come, but neither George nor Thurmond acknowledged her. "Hello, Thurmond. It's me, Nyssa." If she was having trouble recognizing her former neighbors, maybe Thurmond wasn't able to place her, either.

His voice came like the creaking of a nail being pulled out of wood, slow and rasping and indistinct: "Nyssa."

She nodded. Then, because he said nothing more and she thought maybe he wasn't actually watching her from beneath his half-lowered eyelids, she spoke out loud: "Yes." Her heart sank, from fear that his mind, too, had ceased to work. "From next door," she explained, when he said nothing after that simple, earlier repetition of her name. And, when he still said nothing, she added, "Well, not anymore."

"Should hope not," Thurmond said, his voice slurred. He paused between each word, as though needing to recover his strength for the next, and the right half of his face didn't seem to be keeping up with the left. "Household of thieves there." His right hand fluttered, a smooth and flaccid hand, unlike a woodworker's hands with their cuts and nicks and calluses. "Thieves," he repeated, saying the word more loudly this time, at the cost of being less clear. There was a time when his voice could have carried most of the way down the block, calling for Rufus—or George—shouting out a greeting, laughing: it made no difference whether at his own joke or someone else's. If he meant for the two workers next door to hear him calling them thieves, Nyssa doubted they could.

George glanced up from his work only long enough to say mildly, "Don't get him overly excited. He drools all over himself, and then somebody's got to clean him up."

Thurmond jerked his head in the direction of Nyssa's old house. "Thieves," he repeated. He managed to tip his head up, indicating George behind him. "Moron. Not sure which is worse."

This was more like the Thurmond she used to know. She wanted to encourage him, to let him know she saw that his mind was sharp, just trapped in a body that didn't work. Her mother used to hug people, to pat their hands in encouragement, to rub their shoulders to show sympathy. As much as Nyssa had enjoyed such physical comforting, as much as she had wished she could be more like her mother, she had always felt awkward around people. She was sure such attempts on her part appeared forced and insincere and would reveal her as a shallow fraud attempting to be genial. She looked down at Thurmond's hand, pale and still flapping, and could not bring herself to touch it.

She crouched down before him. "Thurmond," she said, "Elsdon is back."

She could see him struggle to get the words out.

"I'd spit," Thurmond told her in his slow, one-word-at-a-time, ruined voice, "but I'd get it all over me. And he'd—" once again he flung his head back to indicate George, "—think I did it just to spite him."

"Elsdon got away with killing my parents."

Thurmond nodded. His eyes were still half closed, but she knew he was listening and thinking.

"I want him to pay," Nyssa said.

Thurmond nodded again. "Spoke to the magistrates," he said, "back then. Back ten years ago."

It had been only six, but Nyssa granted that the date was more important to her than to anyone else.

"You saw him," she insisted.

"Heard your mother scream," Thurmond said,

the same thing he'd said on the street after it had happened, and again as sworn testimony. "Saw Elsdon running. Figured she'd caught him peeking. Never thought it was worse till I heard *you.*"

Thurmond's hand flopped some more in his lap. Nyssa didn't know if *he* wanted to pat *her* hand in comfort, or if he was trying to demonstrate something, or if he was just agitated.

He gathered enough strength to ask, "Who's a magistrate going to believe—me or them?"

Them would be Lord Haraford and Lady Eleanor, who'd sworn Elsdon had been home that evening.

Thurmond was right about the magistrates. And if they hadn't believed him when he stood upright and spoke in his booming voice, there was no reason to hope they would believe him now.

To Nyssa's horror, Thurmond began to shake, and she was sure some sort of fit had come upon him. He gave a choked cry. Tears began to leak from his eyes. "So sorry," he said, his words even more garbled than before, "so sorry about your poor family." As a result of his agitation, he did indeed begin to—as George had foretold—drool. "Life's been cruel to both of us."

Behind him, George set down the plane. "For the love of the saints," he muttered.

Hastily Nyssa pulled her sleeve down over her wrist and used the material to blot at Thurmond's face. "He's all right," she assured George so he wouldn't get angry. "He's fine."

George shook his head but returned to his work.

Thurmond, unfortunately, continued to cry.

"Don't worry," Nyssa assured him. "I'll get him. Somehow or other I'll prove Elsdon is the guilty man."

But then Thurmond said, "My legs . . . my poor legs . . ." and Nyssa realized that she was being witless again—single-mindedly seeing everything only as it related to her and to her parents' murder—while Thurmond had moved on to anguish over his own problems.

George said, "Maybe it would be best if you left now."

Nyssa hesitated. Thurmond had often complained about George's willfulness and his temper. But George didn't sound angry now—at least she didn't think so. She didn't believe George would take out his frustration at Thurmond's helplessness on Thurmond.

"I'm sorry," she said, getting up, then backing away. "I didn't mean to cause harm . . ."

Thurmond wasn't getting coherent words out anymore; and George, back to work inside his shop, absently waved her away. "He'll get over it," he said. "Everybody eventually gets over everything, one way or another."

Ominous as that sounded to Nyssa, she picked up her pole and buckets and headed, finally, toward the well.

Five

Nyssa had not blotted Thurmond's tears with intent to use them for her own purposes.

But that night, lying in bed, she was unable to reach Elsdon's dreams. Over and over she drifted off to sleep, only to awake later in the night, having dreamed nothing beyond the jumbled thoughts and fragments that she might have had on any normal, restless night. Elsdon was not permitting himself to sleep. Elsdon did not want to risk having his guilty conscience catch up to him.

Once again, she had a picture of him so clearly in her mind, sitting with his arms wrapped protectively about himself, that she almost could have believed that she was, in fact, still asleep and that this was a true-memory dream. But she knew it wasn't.

Nyssa crawled out of bed, causing Peldrida and Maddy's annoyed bestirrings, and she fetched her dress from the nail by the door. She took Elsdon's coin out from under her pillow and hid it under the mattress to use on another night; then she folded her dress beneath her pillow so that its sleeve edge that still held Thurmond's dried tears was the closest thing to where her head would lie.

Any smart person would have thought of it before: to get some token from the only witness—to experience, exactly, what he had experienced.

Nyssa fell asleep, and cool, soft, wish-dream ripples washed over her.

Thurmond is running, but it is not a frantic fleeing. He is exalting in being young—Nyssa guesses that he's picturing himself as he was at about age twenty—and he has young, healthy, strong legs. These legs carry him at a fast speed through an endless meadow simply for the joy of covering ground, of feeling the soft grass give way beneath him, of knowing he can outdistance any trouble or sorrow.

Thurmond spies a pretty, young woman in the middle distance of the meadow, and she's obviously delighted to see him. She waves both arms in greeting, but she stays where she is, letting him show off his powerful, tireless legs, letting him come to her.

Nyssa does not remember Thurmond's wife, Avis, who died giving birth to a dead baby when Nyssa was very young, but that is who Thurmond's sleeping mind tells her this is.

Thurmond catches Avis up in his arms and spins her around and around and around in the golden air.

When he finally sets her down and looks deep into her laughing face, her sparkling eyes, they join hands and run together through the meadow, running, running, running. . . .

Nyssa woke up crying, which—she told herself—

just went to show how foolish she could be. This was not a sad dream; it was a happy dream. *Life* was what was sad.

Peldrida reached over and patted her shoulder. "'Sall right," she reassured Nyssa sleepily.

Nyssa wiped her eyes with her hands and forced herself to lie still.

In another few moments the tears stopped altogether. This time Nyssa used the edge of the blanket to wipe her face. Then she fell back to sleep.

Thurmond's next dream started with the unnatural clarity of true memory.

Thurmond is in his shop, straddling the lesser workbench, the bench that should be the apprentice's workstation. The air is fragrant with freshly worked wood and the oil of Thurmond's well-tended instruments. There are a bunch of spokes before him, and he is going over them very carefully with a spokeshave, making minute adjustments. "See," he is telling his nephew George, a young apprentice once again, "like this. Rounded. A spoke is supposed to be perfectly rounded."

Rufus, barely more than a puppy, tries to catch the curls and flakes that fall from Thurmond's shave.

"They ARE rounded," George replies sulkily. He has his arms crossed in front of his chest. He seems to be having trouble standing still, impatient and obviously resentful of either the woodworking lesson or Thurmond's patronizing tone.

Rufus barks at George.

"They're ALMOST rounded," Thurmond corrects,

ignoring George's tone and his mood.

"They're rounded ENOUGH."

That certainly gets Thurmond's attention. "You," he says crisply, "are the apprentice. I am the master woodworker—"

Rufus, who can sense the tension between them, barks.

George has had one booted foot up against the leg of the table lathe. Now he lets the foot drop with a thud. "Yes, yes," he interrupts Thurmond, who has raised his voice to be heard above Rufus. "I'm sure your customers are all quite the discerning experts on such matters."

Thurmond's face is getting redder, and his voice is getting louder. "The rounder the spokes, the more efficient the wheel."

George comes right out and shouts, "Anyone who is that concerned with an efficient wheel is buying that wheel about seven shops farther up the street."

"When I told my sister I'd take you in . . ."

This is obviously the start of a story George has heard before. He throws his hands up into the air and heads for the front door, the one that leads out of the shop and into the street rather than the one that goes back into the house.

Thurmond yells after him, "The neighborhood women have been complaining about you!"

George strides through the door without answering.

Rufus follows him to the door, barking his comments after him.

When Thurmond gets to the door, there's a customer standing there, who has already been almost run down by George and is now reluctant to take on Rufus. He backs away as Thurmond yells after George, "You need to get your mind off your pants and onto your work!"

Without any indication that he's heard, George continues walking down the street, past Nyssa's own house.

Somewhat apprehensively, gazing from angry woodworker to barking dog, the customer says to Thurmond, "Maybe now is not a good time?"

"Rufus!" Thurmond commands the still-barking dog and returns to the workbench, the dog following at his master's feet.

The customer sticks only his head into the shop, maybe suspecting that a speedy retreat might still be needed. He asks Thurmond, "Those the spokes?"

Thurmond hesitates, then says, "They're almost ready." He sits back down and completes the work himself.

He packages up the finished spokes, hands them to the man, accepts his money.

Since the day is almost over, he is putting things away, cleaning up tools and work surfaces, when Rufus, standing with his paws up on the side window that faces Nyssa's father's shop, starts barking.

"Rufus!" Thurmond commands.

The dog looks over his shoulder at his master, but does not come. He resumes barking.

Thurmond congratulates himself for having nailed one shutter in place, making the window too small for Rufus to squeeze through, which he has done on more than one occasion to the irritation of neighbors.

From next door comes a scream.

Rufus barks more frantically.

Thurmond lets drop the vise he was about to put away and runs to the door just in time to see young Lord Elsdon run out from between the two buildings, away from the window at the side of Nyssa's father's shop.

"Hey!" Thurmond calls after him.

Elsdon keeps on running.

"Rufus!" Thurmond orders. "Stop." He shakes his head. He mutters to himself, "At least George isn't the only young fool around here bothering the women."

Rufus, after wavering between Thurmond and the window, stays at the window, still barking.

Thurmond slams the outside door shut and once more resumes putting his tools away for the night.

Nyssa sat up in bed, rocking back and forth, unable to control her shivering.

She had never before known how it had happened. She knew that Elsdon had ordered a wooden box for his mother's birthday. He had come back several times over a three-day period, apparently never satisfied. Nyssa had worked out two possibilities.

The first was that Elsdon had come this day, too, and that Father had left Mother to show him the latest changes in the hope that Elsdon would not dispute the price or the workmanship with her. Maybe Elsdon had really wanted the box, or maybe he had been more interested in Mother. Whatever his reason for visiting their shop, on this day he had made advances toward Mother. She had resisted, which would explain why the shop had been in disarray, but finally she had managed to scream—the scream Nyssa and Worrell, in the backyard, had heard. Angry or panicked, Elsdon had picked up a chisel from Father's workbench and had stabbed her with it. When Father had come running to Mother's rescue, Elsdon had bashed him on the head with a mallet hard enough to kill him, too. By then Worrell had come in, and Elsdon had hit him also before making his escape.

The other possibility she had worked out was that Father and Elsdon had quarreled, which had led to a struggle. In this version, Mother must have heard the disturbance and had walked in just after Elsdon had struck Father the killing blow. Mother screamed, so Elsdon killed her, too. Then Elsdon had lingered, possibly looking for money or for the box Father had fashioned for him. Maybe he had been cleaning Mother's blood off himself so no one on the street would guess what he had just done. For whatever reason, he had delayed long enough for Worrell to come bursting in from the backyard.

But no, Nyssa now realized. It couldn't have happened either of those ways. There was not nearly enough time.

Thurmond had always said he'd run to the door after Mother's scream. But now, having seen his true memory of that evening, Nyssa realized what a short amount of time had passed between Thurmond's hearing Mother's scream and his seeing Elsdon run away. And there had been no blood on Elsdon, not on his hands, not on his clothes—despite all the blood on Mother and on the floor.

He didn't have time, Nyssa realized, to have

killed Mother, to have wiped the blood off himself, and to have scrambled out the window and started running—all in the time it took Thurmond to go from his workbench to his door. And Elsdon had certainly not lingered long enough for Worrell to come in.

Elsdon hadn't killed them.

All these years he'd been telling the truth.

Well, at least part of it.

He hadn't killed her parents, but he must have seen who had.

Six

Nyssa put a hand to her mouth to stifle a groan.

Always the sympathetic one, Maddy yanked the blanket back up around her and complained, "If you're going to be sick, get out of bed first."

Nyssa hadn't felt she was going to be sick, but once Maddy's words put the thought into her head, she was sure she was about to be. She rolled over Peldrida—convinced there was no time to work her way out over the foot of the bed.

Peldrida curled to protect herself from Nyssa's elbows and knees, which put Nyssa off balance so that—with her foot caught in the blanket—she half fell out of the bed, taking most of the blanket with her.

"Nyssa!" Maddy complained.

"Shh!" Peldrida warned, for if they woke up the rest of the household, Mistress Kermillie would be furious.

Nyssa knelt on the floor but in the end didn't vomit, didn't even gag despite the fact that her world had just turned upside down.

Maddy or Peldrida yanked the blanket back up onto the bed.

Still, Nyssa waited to see if she would be sick. . . .

No, apparently not.

Shakily she got back to her feet. She leaned over Peldrida to reach under her own pillow and whipped out her dress. She pulled it on over her head and put on her shoes. Neither Peldrida nor Maddy said anything, though their breathing, loud and annoyed, clearly indicated they were still awake.

In the kitchen, Nyssa didn't open the shutters to check if it was almost dawn, and never even thought about taking the pole and the well buckets. She simply opened the door and walked out into the street.

Nyssa could see just the faintest hint of pink in the east as she started running. She had no particular place that she was heading—where *was* there for a witless, worthless girl to go who was also selfish, greedy, and heedless? And who had built the last several years of her life on a lie.

She just wanted to keep moving—like Thurmond in his wish dream: Thurmond trying to outrun disaster. She hadn't been able to outrun disaster—she'd run smack into it.

As she approached East Bridge behind the mill, the easternmost of the four bridges that crossed the river in the vicinity of Lindenwolde, she made out two figures on the bridge, one short, one tall, both with fishing lines in hand. The tall one wore a familiar blue, linen shirt, one she had watched her mother make.

Nyssa threw herself into her brother's arms, sobbing.

Somehow Worrell had gotten the fishing line down before she'd reached him, and he rocked her in his arms, making gentle, shushing, everything's-all-right sounds. His young, towheaded son watched her with a certain mild apprehension, but he didn't say anything. He was pretty much a silent lad.

Worrell got her to sit down, his arms around her making her feel safe, though she knew the world had gotten more complicated than that.

"He didn't do it," Nyssa finally managed to get out. "He couldn't have done it."

Worrell raised an eyebrow and waited patiently.

She wiped her nose on her sleeve. "I bespelled Thurmond's dreams," she said.

"Oh, Nyssa." Worrell sighed. "One of these days, you *will* get caught."

"That's not the point," she objected. "You're not listening to me."

"I'm listening," Worrell insisted gently.

Nyssa took a shaky breath. She wasn't being fair. Worrell always listened. Though she had not heard the church bell ring, it must have, since the sun had cleared the horizon and there was enough light for her to see the concern on her brother's face. She said, "I dreamed I was with Thurmond in his shop. He heard Mother scream. He went to the door. He saw Elsdon running away."

Worrell waited, listening, for there was nothing new in this information.

"There wasn't enough time for Elsdon to have murdered Mother, between the time she screamed and when Elsdon climbed through the window. Elsdon definitely didn't stay long enough to attack you." She shook her head. "It must have been someone else—someone Elsdon saw." She took a deep breath. "You saw him, too."

Worrell got that pained look he always did when she asked him to remember that day. He touched the scar on his forehead. "Nyssa, I can't," he said.

"I know," she told him. She sighed. "It's all right."

He looked agitated. Sometimes when he got unsettled or confused, he would disappear for days. Allowances had to be made for Worrell. Since his head injury, he was a lot more fragile than he'd been before.

"I'm not asking you to remember. I'm just trying to work everything out."

He still had his arm around her shoulder, but lightly, as though he was ready to bolt.

She forced jolliness into her tone. "You know how sometimes when you see someone who can read, but he can't read well, when he's reading to himself his lips move because he's sounding the words out to himself? That's the way I think, by sounding things out. I'm not asking you to try to remember."

Worrell gave a wan smile, but at least he stayed where he was.

Nyssa reiterated what they knew: "We were in the backyard together. We heard Mother scream. You ran in right away. Elsdon was probably halfway to Coopers' Square by then, so he didn't see you get hit. But he must have seen . . ." After all these years, she still couldn't bring herself to say, "seen Mother get stabbed." She could talk about Father being killed, but that was the limit of her ability. She shifted her sentence to, ". . . seen who the intruder was." Then she added, "—though the intruder probably didn't see Elsdon, or he would have gone after him to prevent him from saying anything to anybody."

But Elsdon *hadn't* said anything to anybody. Was that because the murderer was someone Elsdon wanted to protect? Was that why Elsdon had been watching her yesterday, to try to intimidate her into silence?

That couldn't be it because he had been away for six years. Six years in which she might have discovered who had attacked her family. So Elsdon couldn't have been *that* concerned about this maybe-person's well-being. From the time Nyssa had been ten, she had publicly made clear her opinion that *Elsdon* was the murderer. Surely this must have caused him *some* inconvenience. She had assumed that was why he had left, to get away from her accusations, the townsfolks' suspicions. Why had he never come forward with what he knew? And why had he returned home now? None of it made any sense.

"It couldn't have been a stranger," Nyssa said, "else why wouldn't Elsdon have said that?"

Worrell watched her without saying a word.

It had always seemed likely that Father must have been the intruder's intended target: Father was argumentative, secretive, prone to rub people the wrong way. The magistrates, though sympathetic to Nyssa, had hinted that it had been just a matter of time before *someone* picked up one of Father's tools, a mallet in this case, and brought it down on his head. And Mother, poor, beautiful, kind Mother, had simply been eliminated as a witness.

But maybe that wasn't the order in which it had happened. Maybe the intruder had come in to steal what little the family had, Mother had seen him and screamed, the intruder had killed her, then had killed Father when he came rushing in to his wife's aid, then had waited for Worrell. . . .

Except that there'd been no time.

Seeing Thurmond's true-memory dream had eliminated possibilities and had left nothing with which to replace them.

It was all too much for a witless girl to sort out.

"So Elsdon can't be the one, then," Worrell said, as though working out a theoretical puzzle, rather than his own family's tragedy. Sometimes

Nyssa appreciated his calm objectivity, but it could also be infuriating. Worrell said, "He was telling the truth all along when he said he wasn't the one."

"Well, not exactly the truth," Nyssa pointed out. "He said he was never there. He said he was with his parents."

Worrell's son had given up on the fishing and had pushed his way up under Worrell's arm and into his lap. Worrell was a good father, Nyssa thought, better than their own had been, patient and gentle. Nyssa recognized that her voice had been getting strident and that she had probably been scaring the boy, probably scaring the fish, too.

"But it's the larger truth," Worrell insisted, with his unfailing sense of justice. "There never was any real reason for Elsdon to come after our family."

"He and Father argued," Nyssa reminded him.

"Over the making of a box," Worrell scoffed. "That never seemed likely. Why would a rich lad like that come to a shop like ours for a box? Even if," —he talked over her objection so that their words both tumbled out together, overlapping— "it was to be a surprise for his mother's birthday."

Worrell finished, "Father wouldn't have been able to make him pay for the box if he didn't want to. I'm sure other people have called Elsdon a spoiled, rich brat before. Surely he hasn't gone around killing all of them."

"All right." Nyssa was getting annoyed that Worrell was making the issue more complicated, rather than helping her think it out. *She* was the one of slow wit. Father had always said so. Worrell, he had called clumsy. Except that in Worrell's case, Father had been wrong. Still, why wasn't Worrell coming up with solutions? "Elsdon was at the shop that day as well as several days before, for whatever reason. Now we know that isn't important because—*apparently*—Elsdon didn't do it, couldn't have done it, had no time to do it, as well as having no reason to do it."

Worrell rested his chin on his son's head, watching her appraisingly. As though—damn him!—he was enjoying this. He was enjoying her being forced to think. Which *might* have been a fine joke *if* the question at hand wasn't who had killed their parents.

Worrell saw she was getting distracted and put the question to her: "So, if not Elsdon, who?"

"Obviously I don't know," she snapped. "It would help if you could tell me who you saw that day."

That was an unfair blow. He momentarily closed his eyes, and his hand instinctively went to the scar on his forehead, as though it pained him still. He shook his head, for once as mute as his mute son.

"I'm sorry," she said. "It's just I was so sure it was Elsdon." She remembered Elsdon's fear dream of being buried alive. She told her brother, "He has a guilty conscience about something."

Worrell snorted. "Who doesn't?"

He was going to leave her to work it out on her

own. If he thought he was helping her to become smarter, more independent, it was just plain frustrating.

Nyssa continued, "Thurmond always claimed that, when he first heard Mother scream and then saw Elsdon running away, his original thought was that Mother had caught Elsdon spying through her window. It was only after Thurmond learned Mother and Father had been killed that he decided *that* was what Elsdon must have been doing."

"So what does that tell you?" Worrell asked.

Nyssa considered. "That, maybe, Thurmond was wishing Elsdon was guilty. . . ."

She was speaking so slowly that Worrell, looking skeptical, prompted her, "Because . . . ?"

"Because . . . in his heart he suspected his nephew, George, had done it?"

Worrell looked amazed. "Why George?"

"Apparently George was one who *did* like looking into women's windows. In Thurmond's dream, George had left Thurmond's shop, and he had enough time to walk down the street and back. Maybe Father caught him looking at Mother . . ."

Worrell was looking very skeptical.

". . . they got into a fight . . . *Could* it have been George?"

Worrell shook his head in exasperation. Slowly, distinctly, he asked, "Nyssa, for what reason?"

Why, she wondered, had Thurmond dreamed of his argument with George unless it was important?

Of course the fact that it was important to Thurmond didn't necessarily mean that it had any connection to Nyssa and her family.

"I will get more information," she assured Worrell, "before I accuse anyone."

"What about your job?" he asked. "What about Mistress Kermillie?"

It was past dawn. The wool merchant's household would be up. Surely the mistress would have noticed her absence by now.

Nyssa hiked her skirt up and ran all the way to Wool Street without once looking over her shoulder to see if Worrell and his son had resumed their fishing.

She was concentrating so much on getting back that she didn't see Elsdon until she passed right by him, sitting alone once more at Barlow's tavern across the street. She passed so close, he could have grabbed her, except that he'd been too absorbed in watching the doors of Master Darton's home and shop, and he didn't notice her, either, until she dashed across the street.

He'd gone beyond looking haggard. With lack of sleep, his face was pale, and he had dark circles under his eyes. He appeared on edge, desperate. Dangerous. She would have thought so even if she hadn't heard the scrape of his bench as he pushed back from the table.

Sure that he was pursuing her, she almost ran down a man selling hot pastries in her hurry to get inside Mistress Kermillie's. She slammed the door shut behind her, then leaned against it, breathing heavily. Surely Elsdon wouldn't come knocking on the door, demanding to speak to her.

Or at least she hoped not.

She pressed her ear to the door to find out if he'd followed her. But with her heart beating so loudly and her breath coming in ragged gasps, she couldn't hear anything. She opened the door the tiniest crack, ready to take off Elsdon's fingers if he was there and trying to get in.

He wasn't. She opened the door just the tiniest bit more to check if he'd returned to the other side of the street.

He jammed his foot in the door, preventing her from closing it, no matter how hard she pushed. "I will not let you be the death of me," he told her from between clenched teeth.

That was exactly what she'd wanted these past years, to have him die for his crimes. Six years ago she'd publicly accused him, and she had continued to accuse him even after the magistrates had declared him innocent. But why was he reacting so strongly to her now? She'd stayed away from his house since the day before, and there was nothing to link her to his nightmare.

Unless he'd gone as crazy as people seemed to think she was.

She leaned close to the door to whisper, "I haven't done anything."

"Witch," Elsdon said.

It was almost enough to stop Nyssa's heart.

Surely he couldn't know. Surely it was just a wild guess or even just an attempt to intimidate her into her best behavior.

From behind her, Mistress Kermillie said, "Well! So you've decided to return after all. You idle, little layabout, you'd better have a good explanation."

Nyssa thought Elsdon would force his way in and denounce her in front of the mistress. But he must have determined the threat was enough for his purposes. At least for now.

He slid his foot out of the doorway, letting the door shut with a solid thump.

Seven

Nyssa was willing to tell Mistress Kermillie that she had run down to the river because she had felt ill and had not wanted to disturb the household. The rest, as far as Nyssa was concerned, was nobody's business.

"You wouldn't have disturbed us in the backyard," Kermillie pointed out. She sent odious, young master Finn to fetch a switch; but when he offered to administer the beating, she took the switch from him.

"Be aware that I do this for your own good," Kermillie said, as she brought the switch down on Nyssa's bottom. "I'll stop when you thank me."

"Thank you," Nyssa said, but apparently too quickly, or not sincerely enough, for Kermillie didn't stop right away.

For the rest of the morning, Nyssa went about her chores quietly and stiffly and with downcast eyes, the picture of someone who had learned her lesson.

But when Kermillie told her to bring refreshments into the shop because Master Darton's biggest wool supplier was visiting, Nyssa, wearing her best meek and obedient face and attitude, set the tray on the table between them and then kept right on walking out the front door.

She didn't know what she would have done if Elsdon were still in the neighborhood, but she caught no sight of him.

I'll never go back to Mistress Kermillie, she promised herself. It had been bad enough to accept a beating from Father. Now she would rather enter that abbey with which Father had threatened her than return to the wool merchant's house.

She went back to Woodworkers' Street. The two men who shared her father's shop had finished the chest they had been working on the previous day and were loading it onto a wagon. Rufus was barking at them and at the horse that waited patiently in its traces. Thurmond was once again propped up in his chair on the stoop, though George had his door closed, perhaps against the noise, or maybe he was eating his midday meal, or maybe he didn't have any business that day.

Nyssa went to the house across the street, the house of Leoma, who had been her mother's best friend.

"Nyssa!" Leoma greeted her with a hug that, though a bit smothering due to Leoma's immense size, felt surprisingly good. Leoma put out two cups of wine, a tray of fruit, and a bowl of hazelnuts, as though Nyssa, too, were an important wool merchant's important supplier. "You poor, sweet honey," Leoma said. "It's been too long since I've seen you. You look too thin. How have you been?"

"I've been well," Nyssa assured her, not wanting to go into why she was having trouble sitting. *Everyone* was thin by Leoma's standards. "But I've been thinking about my parents. . . ."

Leoma shook her head and clicked her tongue. "Such a tragedy. Such a senseless tragedy. Not that it would have brought your poor family back, but if only the one who had done it had been brought to justice . . ." Again she shook her head. She made the sign of the cross. "If not in this world, in the next." She indicated for Nyssa to try the grapes.

Ignoring the food, Nyssa said, "I used to think Lord Elsdon had done it."

"I know you did, my dear. You were always quite vocal about that." Nyssa found herself blushing, even though Leoma was continuing, "And, frankly, I always believed you may well have been right. Thurmond was quite adamant that he'd seen young Elsdon running away from between the shops directly after your poor, dear mother screamed. Have you visited Thurmond lately?" She didn't give Nyssa a chance to answer but added, "Such a shame, such a shame. And I was one of the ones who saw him the day before. Elsdon, not Thurmond. I saw *Elsdon* loitering about the shops at this end of the street. 'No good is going to come of that,' I told myself. But, Nyssa," —she shook her finger for emphasis—"it's over now. They've declared Elsdon innocent, and you will only bring trouble down upon yourself if you harass him." Once again she cut off any possible reply from Nyssa. "I'm assuming you've heard that he's back from staying with his uncle or his mother's cousin or wherever it was they sent him off to. And I'm as sure as you that they sent him away precisely to keep him out of the public eye lest that old accusation come back to haunt them. Perjured themselves, did Lord Haraford and Lady Eleanor, claiming he was with them all the time. Still, that one may yet come to do something his parents' wealth can't protect him from. I've heard rumors." Leoma *always* heard rumors because she vigorously hunted them down. She finished, "But *you* must be above reproach, Nyssa."

"Yes." Nyssa was finally able to get a word in. She didn't ask what kind of rumors Leoma had heard about Elsdon, because she had not come here to learn about him. She said, "Well, I'm no longer convinced Elsdon is the one who did it."

"Nyssa," Leoma said, with a stern look, "I have the feeling this doesn't bode well."

"Why?" Nyssa asked innocently.

"One," Leoma counted off on her finger, "because I've heard the young women about town fairly *buzzing* about how handsome young Elsdon has grown to be, and I thought you had more sense than that."

"No!" Nyssa protested, but then realized that sounded as though she was affirming that no, she didn't have more sense than to be swayed by

Elsdon's good looks. "I mean, no, that isn't why I've changed my mind. I don't care how he looks. He's . . . He's . . . All right, he's *presentable,* but what do his looks have to do with me? How could you ever think I could be that . . . that . . . ?" The word she was trying to avoid was *witless.*

"Because,"—Leoma switched to her second finger—"that would be better than thinking you're about to get involved with accusing someone else. Nyssa, I'm remembering last time, how overwrought you became, screaming and crying and threatening."

"Like a madwoman," Nyssa admitted.

"Like a mad child," Leoma corrected. "You were, what? Ten?"

Nyssa nodded.

"People were willing to take into account that you were a sudden orphan, that you had just seen the bodies of your poor, murdered family. You're fourteen now?"

"Sixteen," Nyssa corrected.

Leoma clicked her tongue disapprovingly. "You're so skinny you look closer to fourteen. Still, a sixteen-year-old is an adult. They will not permit you to act that way again."

"That's what Worrell says, too," Nyssa agreed.

"*Worrell?*" Leoma repeated. "You've been talking to *Worrell*?" Leoma shook her head disapprovingly. There was much that Leoma disapproved of.

"No more screaming," Nyssa assured her.

"No more crying."

"A little bit of crying would be good," Leoma said. "I recommend a good cry at least once every month or so. Twice during my birthday month. Just not loudly, in the middle of the street."

"Yes," Nyssa said, as though that was all settled. She tried to ease the topic back to the one she wanted. "So," she said, "can you please tell me about George?"

"George?" Leoma echoed. "Now it's George you think is to blame?"

Well, maybe she hadn't been as subtle as she'd thought. "No," Nyssa said. "Of course not. But is it true that he looks in women's windows?"

"Well, not mine!" Leoma said so indignantly that Nyssa had to laugh. Leoma looked down at her ample body and said, "It's been a few years since any of the boys were looking in my window."

"But it's something George does?"

"Did," Leoma corrected. "Years ago. There was a roving pack of young hooligans. There is almost every year. But George's group have all long ago outgrown it."

"Do you think he used to watch my mother?"

"Oh, you poor, dear sweetie," Leoma said. "I suppose it's possible. But, really, they were more interested in looking at the girls their own age."

Nyssa realized that just because *she* thought her mother was beautiful didn't mean everyone else did. "I was thinking maybe my father caught him. . . ." Nyssa drifted off because Leoma was shaking her head.

"I'm not going to say it's impossible, dearie," Leoma said. "But I honestly don't think it very likely. George and the others, they mostly hung about Litton Tanner's house, with his five daughters, none of whom minded, regardless of what they told their mother, or they would have learned to leave the shutters closed. Your mother was truly a lovely woman, but really, dear, George was hardly more than a boy."

Nyssa sighed. It still could be George, for some other reason she hadn't yet thought of. She planned to visit Litton in Tanners' Alley to see if any of the daughters still lived there and if any of them could recall whether George had been there on a certain day, six years ago. It was possible, she told herself. They would have heard of the murders; the day would have stuck in their minds. Possibly.

"If anybody was interested in your mother," Leoma said, "it was Thurmond."

"Thurmond?" Nyssa echoed.

"Certainly. Thurmond and your father both wooed your mother. She chose your father . . ." There was the slightest hesitation, as though Leoma was about to comment on that choice but decided against it. ". . . and Thurmond wed Avis. Then Avis died." Leoma shook the bowl of hazelnuts to spread them out better since her side of the bowl was getting considerably lower than Nyssa's.

This was not one of the family stories anyone had ever shared with Nyssa before.

It couldn't have been Thurmond, she thought. She'd seen him in the true-memory dream, hearing her mother cry out.

But he could have hired someone to kill Father, she supposed. Killing Mother couldn't have been part of Thurmond's plan, not if he wanted a second chance to win her. But this hypothetical hired murderer could have killed Mother *despite* Thurmond's wishes, perhaps because she had caught him in the act of killing Father.

And maybe Thurmond *had* ordered Mother's death. Maybe he was less interested in winning her back and more interested in retaliating for her not choosing him.

Nyssa feared her mind was clutching at ideas that were more and more far-fetched.

Worrell kept trying to get her to think about this sensibly: who would gain by the death of either her father or her mother?

She asked, "What about the men who own my father's shop now?"

"Kleef and Merritt," Leoma said. "I don't think they even knew your mother, dear."

"Did they know my father? Did they have any grudge against him?"

Leoma sighed. "A lot of people had grudges against your father, Nyssa—half the Woodcrafters' Guild and most of the neighbors."

There were miles between grudges and murder.

Nyssa pressed, "Were those two able to get the shop because my father was dead?"

"They could have bought him out as easily as they bought the shop from the guild."

Still, Nyssa thought. *Still* . . . Thurmond had called them thieves—although that could be for displaying what Father used to call just plain, good business sense. But this was something to look into, along with visiting the headquarters of the Woodcrafters' Guild to ask if anyone had had a particular animosity toward her father.

Now that she had a plan, Nyssa was eager to finish her visit. But Leoma wouldn't be satisfied until she told Nyssa all about Thurmond's accident last year—which Nyssa already knew about. And about the woman next door who had given birth to twins—very unlucky, even though both mother and children seemed to be doing well, at least so far. And about the doings of everyone who had lived on the street when Nyssa had lived there six years earlier, and about the doings of everyone who had moved there since.

When Nyssa was finally able to get away from Leoma, she headed off toward the town center, because she was sure that Leoma, who always wanted to know everything, was watching.

But then she circled back.

Thurmond was still on the stoop in front of George's closed door. Nyssa walked between their shop and their neighbors', then into the backyard, thinking that she would approach her old house from behind. She had no idea what she expected to find after six years, but George and the boys weren't the only ones who could look through windows.

Rufus, however, came running up to her, barking exuberantly, which was sure to alert everyone.

"Shh," Nyssa said. She knelt to pet the dog to quiet him. "Shh, Rufus."

Rufus lay down on his back, exposing his belly.

Nyssa took the time to scratch him, but then he suddenly twisted around and jumped to his feet, barking once more—not at her now, but at someone behind her.

Before she could turn, a shadow fell over her, then someone seized hold of her, both arms tight around her, a hand clapped over her mouth. "Don't scream," a man's voice warned.

But why wouldn't she be inclined to scream when someone sneaked up behind her, grabbed her, muffled her, and told her not to scream?

She screamed into his hand, which didn't produce much sound at all, so she switched to trying to bite him, but she couldn't really get hold of any flesh. She twisted and threw her weight forward, hoping to unbalance her assailant, but he anticipated this move and not only stayed on his feet but didn't loosen his hold on her.

"Stop struggling," he hissed into her ear.

Rufus continued to bark, circling, lunging forward, then pulling back, apparently unable to decide whether all this activity was fighting that needed his intervention or playing that needed his joining in.

"I'm not going to hurt you," said the man behind her, "not unless you make me."

Make you? Nyssa thought, furious that he implied she was to blame.

Still, he hadn't hurt her so far, though Nyssa guessed he could easily have used more force if he had chosen to. Of course that didn't mean he wouldn't later on. "I just want to talk," he assured her.

Nyssa thought, *Talk after you let go,* and she brought her foot down as hard as she could on his instep.

No reaction. His boots were strong.

He shifted his hold on her, and she knew she couldn't get loose, but she thought she'd fare better if she could just face her assailant—at the least she could see who he was and what he was doing. She managed to twist in his arms.

But, no, that didn't improve the situation at all.

Now she could see that the person who had hold of her was Elsdon.

As if that wasn't bad enough, she could also see that the reason he had been distracted enough so she could wrench herself around was that he'd been getting a knife out of its sheath.

He placed the blade against her throat.

Eight

Elsdon had deteriorated since the last time she'd seen him—his skin paler, the circles under his eyes darker, his cheeks hollowed. But not weak, like a sick man. He had, in fact, too much energy, like a man on the edge of delirium.

"What are you doing?" he demanded.

Nyssa swallowed, aware of the knife against the skin of her throat. "I *was* petting the dog," she said, though she knew that wasn't what he meant. He hadn't been stalking her for the past two days to make light conversation.

His voice shook slightly. "What are you doing to me?"

Nyssa considered for a moment, then said, "*You* are the one who came up behind *me*—"

"What are you doing to my dreams?"

That took Nyssa by surprise. "Nothing." She tried to sound calm, though her heart, which had just begun to slow down after her exertions, started to race again.

"I see you. I see you, at night, casting spells on my dreams."

"No, you don't," Nyssa said. He couldn't. No one could.

He just stood there, watching her with those too-bright eyes.

Thurmond's dog kept circling them, still barking.

That was not helping Elsdon's jumpy nerves.

"Rufus!" Nyssa ordered, and the dog slunk to her side and sat, that just-barely-sitting posture of a dog who would much prefer to be back on his feet. He looked ready to start in again if he decided that something interesting was happening.

And all the while Elsdon continued to silently watch her.

"I can't help what you dream," Nyssa told him, which was only partially true. She certainly had nothing to do with a dream's content; she couldn't even control what kind of dream she called forth—wish, fear, or true memory.

But this was nit-picking. Though Elsdon had the details wrong, he had the gist of it right, and an accusation of witchcraft did not need as solid proof to back it up as an accusation of murder would need. He could kill her, claiming justification because she was a witch, and her own odd and erratic behavior would support his claim. In the eyes of the law, witches needed killing, one way or another.

She felt the blade jitter against her throat as though he'd decided he'd talked long enough, as though he was trying to get up the nerve to press it tightly enough to . . . To what? Slice through skin and arteries? Or was the blade big enough and sharp enough that he might be considering decapitating her? *Not decapitation,* Nyssa mentally begged. In the church there was a tapestry of St. John the Baptist with his head on a platter, and surely having your body in pieces was even worse than simply being dead.

Nyssa closed her eyes, bracing herself.

Elsdon hadn't been the one, she thought. She'd finally figured out he couldn't have murdered her family, but by entering his dreams she had driven him to a point where he was ready to murder her.

The blade moved away from her throat. Not totally away. Elsdon hadn't withdrawn his arm.

Nyssa opened her eyes and saw that the knife was not a finger's width away from her throat.

He hadn't been considering hacking her head off, she decided. The tremor in his arm was just another symptom of two nights without sleep.

She remembered that image she'd had of him after his dream of being buried alive, when she'd imagined him huddled with his arms circled around his knees, afraid to go back to sleep.

The image had been so clear, so real.

That was a guess, she told herself, a conjecture based on her being unable to capture any more of his dreams that night, or the next. Hadn't it?

"I see you," Elsdon insisted. His voice was as shaky as his arm, but Nyssa didn't for a moment think she'd be able to overpower him or outrun him. He said, "I see you lying in bed, casting spells. You share a bed with Master Darton's two other serving women, the heavyset one on your left, the older one on your right."

All that proved was that he knew for whom she worked—which of course he did because he'd been watching her. It proved that at one time or another he had seen all three of them, and the rest was an obvious conclusion based on the size of the house and typical sleeping arrangements. Well, maybe not that obvious. Nyssa tried to work out what the chances were: Peldrida could be on the left, Maddy on the right; that would have been another possibility. Or Peldrida in the middle with Nyssa on the left and Maddy on the right. Or . . . all right, knowing what order they slept in, that *was* a lucky guess.

Elsdon said, "The blanket you share is green, though splotchy as though something went wrong in the dying, which is probably why Darton couldn't sell it and gave it to you three. You keep your dress on a nail by the door; the others have nails closer to the bed—"

Nyssa would have accused him of peeking in their window, except they had an inner room that didn't have a window. He could have paid someone for that information, but for what purpose? She said, not because she meant it, but simply trying to disperse the accusation of witchcraft, "If you see me in a room without windows, then perhaps you're the one who casts spells."

His face went totally white at that, and he moved the knife back in so that it was once again touching her skin.

And in that moment she knew she was right.

He didn't make any denial. Instead he said, "Then perhaps we both do."

He was a witch, too. She *had* seen him those nights. And somehow or other, his witchcraft and hers had combined to link their minds. That's why the vision of him sitting on his bed with his arms around his legs had seemed so real. It *was* real.

Rufus seemed to sense the tension between them and resumed barking.

Then, when it seemed the most unlikely time for it, Elsdon moved the knife away from her, though he didn't loosen his hold on her. He said, "It's not safe speaking like this here, where we might be overheard. We need to talk where we can be alone."

Alone? With him? Where he could kill her without fear of interruption? For now she realized Elsdon's fear dream was about how much he dreaded being found out as a witch. Even though his family was rich and had been able to protect him from her accusations of murder, they wouldn't be able to protect him if people began to suspect he was a witch—any more than her family would have been able to protect her. He knew his life rested in her hands, and that could not have felt like a secure place to be.

There was no reason she should trust him.

But he, too, knew something about spells. It gave them a bond—as strange as that idea was—the half-crazed orphan girl and the son, albeit the youngest son, of the Lord of Lindenwolde.

And she had falsely accused him of murder, had hounded him and his family. She owed him for that.

She said, "I'll go with you. But I want you to know I'm not causing your dreams." To his skeptical look she added, "Truly. Though I do know something of them."

He nodded, apparently willing to wait for the rest. He even put the knife away. But he kept a firm hold on her arm as he led her between the houses and out into the street.

Rufus trotted along beside them, and Nyssa caught hold of the ruff of his neck and led him to where Thurmond sat bound to his chair. "Stay," she commanded.

Rufus whined, and she pressed down on his back end, making him lie at Thurmond's feet. "Stay," she repeated.

She thought that Thurmond, who was watching Elsdon through his half-lowered eyelids, didn't look any more pleased than Rufus did.

"I'll be fine," Nyssa assured him, though she didn't know if she would be, and she wasn't sure in any case that Thurmond really recognized Elsdon—or cared that she was going off with him.

As she and Elsdon walked in silence, she tried to estimate her chances. Could she wrest free of him? Very unlikely. Could she get people's attention by screaming for help? Yes. But whether anyone would come to her aid was another question.

Nyssa remembered that once again she had not combed her hair nor washed her face, making her look the part of the witless girl her father had called her, the crazy girl the townsfolk had come to name her. She checked the skirt of her dress and decided it wasn't too bad, if you didn't count that Rufus had shed all over her.

Of course people would come to help me, she assured herself, even if she had the reputation for being crazy and didn't quite look presentable. *They just probably wouldn't be able to help in time.* For she guessed that if she screamed, Elsdon would probably decide he had nothing left to lose. He would be better off killing her in full view of witnesses rather than letting her accuse him of witchcraft.

She said, "Please keep in mind that I have no way of betraying your secret without giving away my own."

He didn't answer, though she thought she had made an excellent point.

She added, "And I don't believe anymore that you're the one who killed my parents."

"Oh, I'm so relieved," he told her in a flat, definitely un-relieved voice. "I don't believe *you* killed them, either."

Nine

"Where are you taking me?" Nyssa asked as Elsdon led her through Lindenwolde's gates. She had assumed he'd bring her to his father's house rather than the edge of the town.

For a moment it seemed as though he wouldn't answer, then he said, "A hunting blind in the forest."

She balked at that, but his grip on her arm tightened, and he kept moving, pulling her along. She could throw herself to the ground and refuse, but the time for that had been when they were within the town proper, for there wasn't anybody near them at the moment—certainly nobody to intervene if he pulled that knife out again. In fact he could probably kill her here, if he was careful not to get her blood on him, and nobody would be the wiser. Witless, *witless* girl.

Thurmond, she thought. *Thurmond saw us leave together.*

If anybody thought to ask him.

If anybody could understand him.

If anybody believed him.

Elsdon must have seen her panic. He stopped dragging her forward. "I'm not going to hurt you," he told her.

What else would he say?

She tried to convince herself that he seemed calmer, more rational. When he started walking again, she walked also. She said, "When you first saw me two days ago, you made a comment to Ralf. You said, 'She still alive?' Why? Was that a threat?"

"No." He looked genuinely surprised. "No," he repeated. He lowered his voice, though they'd left the town behind and were approaching the line of trees that marked the beginning of the forest. "I knew you were a witch. Back six years ago."

"How?" she interrupted.

But he ignored that and continued with his explanation. "I was amazed that you hadn't gotten yourself killed in the meantime."

When she considered how witless she could be, the fact that she was still alive *was* somewhat amazing.

Elsdon finished, "It was an incredibly rude thing to say. I meant it for Ralf and didn't realize you'd heard. I'm sorry."

The fact that he was well-spoken didn't mean he wouldn't kill her if he had the chance—to get rid of someone who had made his life unpleasant, to get rid of someone he might see as competition, to get rid of someone who could betray him. He wasn't a social outcast the way she was. He wasn't necessarily as relieved as she'd been to find someone else like him.

In fact he'd probably be deeply affronted if he realized she'd just thought of them as being alike.

But still . . . still . . .

Nyssa expected the hunting blind—if he really was taking her to such a place—to be a cramped contraption built of woodland brush. But it was more like a cottage.

Another wave of panic washed over her. Witchcraft aside, he might have wanted to get her alone and beyond help to—as Mistress Kermillie would say in her circumspect way about young women who should have known better—take advantage of her. But Nyssa guessed that she was not the type to drive anyone, particularly someone as rich and good looking as Elsdon was, wild with uncontrollable passion.

He didn't force her inside the blind, which, because of its narrow windows, would be dark. He even let go of her arm.

Not that Nyssa thought she could get far if she decided to run.

There was a bench outside the blind, on the side with the door, and opposite it was a bale of hay. Nyssa figured the hay would be softer on her recently switched behind, so she sat there.

Softer, but prickly—so not a good choice

after all. Nyssa hoped it would turn out to be the worst of her miscalculations.

Elsdon sat across from her, on the bench, and started abruptly, saying, "You've been stalking me."

"No, I haven't," Nyssa protested indignantly. "You were the one with the sudden fascination with Barlow's tavern, and you followed me today to my old house."

"You kept following me, hounding me, six years ago," Elsdon pointed out. Nyssa knew there was no denying that. "Until I left to stay with my uncle. Then, the moment I returned, there you were."

Nyssa remembered him riding past her that morning she had stood outside his parents' house. "That was coincidence," she assured him.

He didn't look convinced. He said, "You say you don't cause my dreams."

"I don't," said Nyssa. She explained, "Most dreams are meaningless. You think about things you've done during the day, lay plans for the next day, but mostly things get all muddled. You dream yourself into embarrassing situations, like showing up at a feast-day celebration wearing only your undergarments. Or you dream of something ridiculous like . . . you walk into the baker's shop and there's a cow standing there wearing the baker's hat, and every time someone comes in, the cow hits that person on the head with a serving spoon and says, 'The season for strawberries does not start in February.'"

Did Elsdon actually look amused for a moment? Or was he now convinced of her insanity? It was hard to read his expression. "I have never had a dream like that," he stated firmly.

Nyssa crossed her arms and glared at him. "Well, it would be very strange if you did. That's my dream. I had it when I was a little girl. I'd asked my mother if we could go to the bakery for a strawberry tart for my birthday, even though my birthday is in February. And later in the day my mother's friend Leoma told a silly story about a headstrong cow on her father's farm when she was growing up. And then my brother, Worrell, got in trouble with my father because he bent a spoon, trying to reach between the steps to get a button I'd lost that had rolled there. But in the dream, everything got all mixed up together. That's the way regular dreams are—and I imagine you have some of that kind even if you *are* sitting there with that superior look on your face."

"Yes," Elsdon admitted, but he kept the superior look.

"Sometimes you know where the pieces of the dream come from," Nyssa said. "And sometimes you don't. But when I bespell people, they don't have their regular jumbled dreams." Elsdon looked about to interrupt, so she hastened to add, "I don't cause them to dream a specific thing, but cause them to have . . . I don't want to call it a more realistic dream, but a more important dream."

"I have no idea what you just said," Elsdon told her.

"There are three kinds of bespelled dreams, and there's no way for me to tell which kind I'll call up. One kind I call a wish dream, where you dream about something you want: something you want to have or something you want to have happen. I would never have dreamed of a strawberry tart in a wish dream, because a strawberry tart was never that important to me. In a wish dream I would dream about something . . . something *more*." And she certainly wasn't going to give him any power over her by sharing anything that personal. "The dream you had the night I was watching was another kind: a fear dream—something you're really afraid of."

Elsdon scoffed. "Being buried alive was not something I had spent a lot of time worrying about until I met you."

"Maybe not exactly," Nyssa said. "But dreams don't always say exactly what they mean." She thought of the coffin closing in on Elsdon. She remembered the grave digger saying Elsdon couldn't be buried in hallowed ground. She should have recognized what the dream was telling him, because her own nightmares told her the same thing. Witches—along with murderers, traitors, and the unbaptized—were not allowed to be buried in the churchyard.

Elsdon lost the superior, mocking look he'd

been wearing. He stood. And crossed his arms. And walked around the little clearing, too agitated to be still. Finally he sat back down, but still he fidgeted. "Yes," he said, though Nyssa hadn't asked a question. He said, "I did not kill your parents."

"I know that," Nyssa assured him. "Now. I truly regret the hardships I caused you by my accusations."

Elsdon seemed to weigh her words before speaking. "What changed your mind?"

"The third kind of dream," Nyssa said. "I call them true-memory dreams. In a true memory, the dreamer re-lives something exactly as it happened. So if I now dreamed about that day when I asked my mother for the strawberry tart, I would see us just as we looked then. I'd hear every word of Leoma's stories, even though in waking life I don't have those memories anymore. I would feel Worrell's arm around me as he said, 'Don't worry—I'll get that button back for you.'"

Elsdon nodded thoughtfully. "Worrell is the brother who . . ." He touched his own forehead.

"Yes," Nyssa said. "Your turn."

Elsdon looked as though he was considering telling her he didn't know what she was talking about, or as though he might simply refuse. "I don't have the ability to affect dreams," he said. "But I have . . ." He hesitated, whether searching for the word or reluctant to speak it. ". . . visions."

He had been able to see her while she was in a windowless room in Master Darton's house. Was that what he meant—that, just as she could see into people's sleeping minds, he could watch them while they were awake? She asked, "What kind of visions?"

"Visions of possibilities . . ."

She waited.

Just as she was about to ask for clarification, he continued, "Visions of the future . . ." Again he hesitated. "But . . . a future that . . . *sometimes* . . . can be changed."

"Sometimes?" Nyssa repeated.

Elsdon shook his head as though to clear it. "Sometimes I can't tell exactly what I'm seeing. I don't recognize the people. I can't tell *when* whatever it is I'm seeing is going to happen—right away or years in the future. Or why. The vision is usually very quick, a momentary glimpse. Sometimes it's something good or neither good nor bad." Again he shook his head. "But most often it's something that should be changed. And . . ." He seemed reluctant to say it. ". . . sometimes . . . I've been able to prevent things from happening."

He paused for so long that Nyssa thought he'd finished all he planned to tell her, when he added, "Sometimes, by trying to stop something, I've caused that very thing to happen." He closed his eyes for a long moment.

The silence stretched between them, with only the rustling of leaves in the breeze, the chirping of a bird, the buzz of insects. The silence was so sharp, Nyssa was almost willing to blurt out how she felt responsible for what had happened to her family. Almost.

When Elsdon opened his eyes again, he said, "You talked about being able to see someone's actual memory."

Nyssa nodded. "I call them true-memory dreams."

"Did you see mine? Is that how you know I didn't kill your family?"

"It wasn't your dream I saw. But the dream of someone who saw you that night." She asked the question she had been dreading: "What did you see when you were looking into the window of my father's shop?"

"I'm not going to tell you."

And she had been feeling sorry for him.

"What?" Nyssa sprang to her feet. "Why not?"

"If you can see my memories," Elsdon said, "see them."

Nyssa was ready to spit in frustration. This was beyond understanding. If he believed she could see his dreams, if he knew it was just a matter of time before she captured them, why was he refusing to tell her?

Was he protecting someone? She remembered how Lord Haraford and Lady Eleanor had sworn Elsdon had been with them that evening. She had assumed that lie had been to protect him, but what if it was to protect one of them?

But that wasn't plausible at all. How did people like the lord and lady even know her parents, much less wish them ill?

"I haven't slept for two days," Elsdon told her. "I'd had bad dreams before, about being discovered, about people chasing me. But never that vivid, that real. And then when I woke up, I could sense you, across the night, watching me, waiting for me to go to sleep again. I thought you had sent the dream, that you were threatening me. And then the next night, I could feel you reaching out to me, trying to grab hold of my mind, so I didn't dare sleep."

"But I've already explained," Nyssa said. "I wasn't trying to give you bad dreams. I was trying to look into your memory."

"This is what I'm saying," Elsdon said. "I was afraid of you before. Now I understand. Look now."

"What?"

"I haven't slept the past two nights. I'm barely able to keep from falling asleep as I stand. If you want to look into my dreams, look."

"Why can't you just tell me?" Nyssa asked.

He hesitated, as though he was considering. But then he shook his head. "No," he said once again.

What was this? What was he planning, or hoping for?

But what choice did she have if she wanted to finally learn the truth?

"All right," Nyssa said. "We both need to be

asleep." Though it was only early afternoon, she had slept badly enough that she, too, was likely to fall asleep if she lay down.

Elsdon glanced at the hunting blind. "It's dark in there."

She judged by the size of the place that there was enough room that they could both sleep there without having to be any closer than they were now. "Just don't try anything," she warned.

"That's the last thing on my mind," he said quickly enough to sting. Which was ridiculous. She had no interest in him: so what if he found her unappealing? So what if he found her repugnant? But then he laid his hand on her arm as though he was going to say something.

"What?" she snapped at him.

He didn't take offense at her tone. "I'm sorry."

Alarm spiders danced on her backbone and in her stomach, and she remembered how far from town they were, how alone she was. No one would miss her. Kermillie might spare a thought wondering what had happened to her, but it would be more in annoyance for having to find another maid than in concern for her welfare.

Elsdon saw the apprehension on her face and immediately let go of her arm. "I don't mean you any harm," he said.

"Then what is it you're sorry for?" she asked.

"Everything," he told her.

Which, if he meant to reassure her, certainly didn't work.

Ten

Nyssa's eyes took a few moments to adjust to the darkness. Each of the four walls had one window, and these were only wide enough to permit the hunters inside to aim and fire an arrow at any game unwary enough to approach. There was just enough of a clearing all around the blind that the hunters could set out bait to entice the animals out from the surrounding trees. A pile of firewood was stacked against one wall in case the night got colder than a hunting party anticipated, and on another wall was a shelf that held four blankets—four was the largest number of people the room could comfortably accommodate—and a flask of water.

Nyssa told Elsdon, "I need something of yours."

He looked suspicious, maybe thinking she was asking for payment.

"A strand of hair, an article of clothing. Something that is yours. I *will* return it."

"You didn't need something up until now."

Nyssa sighed at his suspicion. Obviously she was in more danger from him than he was from her. She said, "I had a shilling of yours before, but in truth a coin doesn't work well—it doesn't carry your . . . your *you*ness very long before it fades. Especially in this case when you did, in fact, throw the coin away for me to pick up. If you want it back before we start, we have to return to town to get it from under the mattress in Master Darton's house." She gave a great, bare-toothed smile to show what she thought of that plan.

Elsdon got the smile off her face in a hurry when he once more removed his knife from his belt.

Nyssa took a quick step away and found the wall at her back.

Elsdon must have seen her terror. "I won't hurt you," he said. "I never would have hurt you. This . . ." He was handing the knife to her, handle end first. ". . . this was only to convince you to come here. I wouldn't really have used it, even if you had refused to come."

Nyssa sincerely hoped he was telling the truth now. She supposed that giving her the knife was meant to put her more at ease, to reassure her that he was not a threat to her. It was saying: here is protection, a weapon in case you feel you need it.

In truth, they both knew he could easily wrest it away from her anytime he wished.

"My grandfather gave this to me ten years ago," he said.

It also showed that he was quick, realizing the longer he'd owned something, the more of *him* it would carry.

The dagger's handle was not as ornate as she would have expected for a lord—maybe because Elsdon was the youngest of Lord Haraford's sons, maybe because the knife had been given to him when he'd been little more than a lad.

After spreading one blanket out on the floor, Nyssa rolled up a second on which to rest her head. She held the dagger beneath this pillow. She was aware of Elsdon, as far away from her as the room would allow, arranging a blanket for himself. As soon as she closed her eyes, she felt her tiredness roll over her. She guessed that Elsdon, too, would have no trouble falling asleep.

The dream is a true-memory dream, but Nyssa can tell right away that it's the wrong memory.

Elsdon is ten years old. He is in the stable, currying a sorrel mare named Queenie, who is one of his favorites. She is sweet tempered and easily pleased—an apple or a carrot is enough to earn her affection. Queenie will be foaling in the next day or so, and Elsdon wants to make sure all is well with her, and he speaks to her in a soft, soothing voice. The stable is warm and snug, smelling of leather accoutrements and well-tended horses. The stableboys are ignoring him, and life is uncomplicated and comfortable.

Then, through the open door, he sees his father and one of his brothers approaching.

Nyssa would not recognize which of Elsdon's two older

brothers this is, but Elsdon's mind identifies the youth as Severin, Elsdon's THIRD older brother. Only now, with this prodding, does Nyssa remember, very vaguely, hearing about him, the firstborn, who died when Nyssa was very little.

Within Elsdon's true-memory dream, she can sense Elsdon himself. She can taste the unease he feels for his father—and the guilt this feeling triggers—for Lord Haraford has little time and less patience for his youngest son, and at his best is a man who is hard to please and easy to provoke. Nyssa senses Elsdon's antipathy toward the other two brothers, whom he has successfully avoided this day, avoided since their favorite sport is to band together to torment him. But toward Severin, she can tell Elsdon feels as she herself does for her brother. Severin is kind. Severin protects him. Severin is as good as Elsdon hopes to ever be.

As Severin and Haraford walk toward the stable, Elsdon positions himself between Queenie and the wall of her stall, not hiding exactly, but not easily seen, for Father is sure to find fault with what Elsdon's doing or how he's doing it. He thinks both how nice it would be to have a chance to spend the day with his brother, and how fortunate that Father hasn't noticed him.

Lord Haraford and his eldest son are calling for a pair of horses so they can go to the woods for some impromptu hunting.

Elsdon waits, quietly, feeling the prickliness of the bale of hay behind his knees, Queenie's warm breath on his arm.

As the servants rush to prepare the horses, Nyssa experiences something she never has before. Even as she is watching Elsdon, feeling his warring emotions as he both wishes to and dreads going with Severin and Haraford, something else happens. She sees a splash of blood on the earth, feels a crack of unbearable pain, hears the cry of a horse, sees Severin's face gray and slick with agony. It happens so fast, she cannot tell what has happened, or be certain in what sequence the impressions occurred.

She realizes that Elsdon has had one of his visions.

He falls forward, causing Queenie to snort and sidestep to avoid him. He is just as disconcerted as Nyssa, just as confused, just as sure as she—she with her knowledge of eleven years later—that Severin is going to die.

Elsdon rushes out from the stall.

Father utters an oath and demands, "What mischief have you been up to, boy, skulking about, hiding, listening? You're getting more like a woman every day with your sneaking ways."

Severin, though just as startled as his father, tousles Elsdon's hair and simply observes, "Quiet feet."

"I saw something," Elsdon says, knowing this is the wrong way to start, knowing Father has gotten irate every time Elsdon has had one of his visions. Father can't seem to settle on whether Elsdon's fancies will bring humiliation on the family for his being feebleminded, or if they will endanger the family because of suspicion of witchcraft.

Elsdon tries to get the words all out in a rush, before Father can tell him to be quiet. And his words tumble all over themselves, making no sense even to himself: "I saw blood, Severin hurt, it has something to do with the horses, maybe, but it's a very, very strong feeling so I think it's coming soon but I don't know what exactly or when. Just don't go out today, tomorrow, either, or maybe the next day just to be safe. And it has to be gone by then; sometimes it just goes away and everything can be all right if you're only careful, just keep inside because I'm pretty sure it was the ground I saw, and if you're inside, whatever it was won't happen."

"What nonsense—" Father starts.

But Severin puts a restraining hand on Haraford's wrist and says, gently, "Elsdon, calm down. Start from the beginning."

But their father is too angry to listen to even his favorite son. "Enough of this nonsense!" he roars. "The boy needs a strong hand, not pampering," and he uses the back of his free hand to smack the side of Elsdon's head.

Elsdon staggers back against the wall.

Queenie whinnies nervously, and the pair of horses that the servants are preparing for the men's hunting excursion stamp nervously.

Before he's even firmly back on his feet, Elsdon resumes pleading that Severin stay home, though every word he speaks reverberates in his aching skull, and he's sure he's about to disgrace himself by vomiting from the pain.

Severin steps between his father and his brother; and Haraford, disgusted, lets himself be deflected.

Still, Elsdon can tell that Severin doesn't take his fears any more seriously than Father does, though Severin tries to calm him.

Elsdon will not be calmed.

"Enough!" Father says again, when the servants have finished preparing the horses.

Elsdon knows his brother doesn't believe in his visions, but still he hopes that Severin will stay simply to humor him.

But Severin chooses to humor Father instead.

Haraford and Severin mount the readied horses, servants and family alike ignoring Elsdon's tears and protests. While Father lets his mount shoulder Elsdon aside, Severin promises to be careful.

Elsdon's skull feels about to split open, but his vision is clear; he has no trouble seeing what happens next.

Severin's horse, perhaps fidgety because of Elsdon's fuss, perhaps merely high-strung from overbreeding, seems skittish and moves diagonally rather than forward. The horse steps on the upcurved tines of a pitchfork someone has left where it definitely does not belong, so that the handle of the pitchfork whips up out of the straw and smacks the horse directly between the eyes. Hurt, but probably more frightened than hurt, the horse rears back with a whinny of terror, then comes down again, this time full force, this time impaling its hoof on the sharp tines. Again the horse rears, and this time Severin is not able to hold on and falls, hard, to the ground. The horse twists in the narrow confines of the stable doorway, the pitchfork still stuck in the softest inside section of its hoof, and then the horse falls also, coming down on Severin.

Severin is screaming. The injured horse is screaming. Haraford's horse is whinnying and rearing so that Father can barely keep his seat. Servants are trying to come to Severin's aid while avoiding the flailing hooves of the downed horse. Elsdon throws himself down over his brother's upper body, placing himself between Severin's head and the frantic thrashing of Severin's horse.

Someone, perhaps Father, perhaps the head groomsman, gives an order, and someone pulls out a knife and slits the artery in the injured horse's neck. Blood spurts with each beat of the panicked creature's pounding heart. While the horse is still in the process of dying, the servants are finally able to pull it off of Severin.

And then, at last, reluctantly, knowing what he is about to see, Elsdon turns his head to see Severin's lower body.

Despite what he sees, he tells Severin that it's not as bad as it feels. Once again his words tumble out, nonstop, hardly making any more sense than when he was trying to warn his brother, but this time he is using the same calming tones he used earlier on the mare.

One of the stableboys goes running to fetch help, but everyone can see that Severin is dying as surely as the horse with the slit throat, which is bleeding out its last on the ground.

Finally dismounted, Haraford is shaking with the fury of his inability to do anything; then he settles on Elsdon. He grabs his youngest son by the scruff of the neck, pulling him off his dying firstborn. He flings Elsdon to the ground. "How could you do that to your own brother?" he demands.

"I didn't—" Elsdon starts, but before he can get any further, Father kicks him, catching him in the ribs.

"Witchcraft!" Father cries.

"I tried to warn him," Elsdon protests. "I didn't cause this to happen; I just saw it."

Father is distracted from witchcraft by Elsdon's talk of causes, and he accuses Elsdon of having caused the accident—of leaving the pitchfork out in the open. He brings his riding crop down on Elsdon again and again.

Nyssa, experiencing all of this, feels no hint of guilt on Elsdon's part for the pitchfork, no memory of having used or seen it earlier. And she is certain he was not the one who left it on the ground. But he does not try to defend himself against his father's blows, because he knows he is guilty nonetheless. If he were smarter, if he were braver, if he were faster—if he were Severin—none of this would have happened. And if his father were to kill him, it would be no more than he deserves.

Nyssa is the only one paying enough attention to note the moment when—beyond Haraford's angry shouts and Elsdon's soft grunts of pain, and behind the backs of the servants watching in fascinated revulsion as father beats son—Severin dies, alone on the stable floor.

Eleven

Nyssa and Elsdon both woke up after the dream, which was not always the case, but was more likely after a disturbing dream.

"I didn't mean for you to see that," Elsdon said. "I wish you wouldn't go poking and sorting around in my head."

In the dim light of the hunting blind she could see him once again sitting up with his arms around himself, just as she'd seen him after the fear dream they had shared. No wonder he had a tendency to hold himself protectively, she thought. The switching she had received from Mistress Kermillie was nothing compared to the beating his father had inflicted. The beatings her own father had given her had never been that severe. She was also beginning to suspect that what she had originally taken for Elsdon's look of disdain might more likely be a look of I-will-not-reveal-my-thoughts-or-my-feelings-and-maybe-people-will-leave-me-alone.

Nyssa said, "I don't choose the dreams."

After a moment, Elsdon gave a curt nod, to

acknowledge he believed her.

"My father didn't strike me," Nyssa said, "well, not very often and only when I deserved it. Mostly he yelled." She felt guilty for having intruded on such a painful memory, on a part of Elsdon's history that had no bearing on what he'd agreed to share with her. She said, "When he first found out about my dreams, he hit me then. My mother told him it wasn't my fault, that I hadn't chosen to be a witch. She tried to protect me." Nyssa didn't finish this thought: that Father had turned on Mother, that he'd said Nyssa's witch blood must come from Mother's side of the family. And he'd slapped Mother, hard enough to bloody her lip. Nyssa's fault.

Elsdon said, "My mother, also, was a bit more sympathetic than my father." Nyssa waited to hear of a warm, comforting moment, but Elsdon only finished, "Mostly, she just sprinkled holy water on me."

"Why did you come back?" Nyssa asked him.

It was none of her business, but he answered anyway. "My father does not have long to live. He has had a hardness in his belly that has grown till now he can't eat at all. And he passes blood, which has gone from occasionally this spring, to continually."

It was, in truth, more than Nyssa had wanted to hear. Thinking back, she realized she'd seen nothing of Lord Haraford in the past weeks, not even a glimpse of him riding through the town.

Elsdon didn't say whether he and his father had reconciled. "When he dies, his estates will be divided among his three surviving sons. I will get his land in Sterling because that is wild country that my brothers have no interest in, and even my father visited it as infrequently as he could get away with. But it's something I'm looking forward to, because no one there knows me—no accusations of witchcraft will greet me there." His face grew grimmer. "Nor hints that I killed my brother out of jealousy."

Nyssa, who had shared his feelings, knew that had not been the case and guessed that of the two accusations, the second hurt more because it was untrue. She added, "And there will be no crazy girl hounding you for murdering her parents."

"You're not crazy," he said. "Just . . ." He must have been weighing the possibilities, to find the one least likely to offend. He finished, ". . . a bit overly persistent."

Persistent. Nyssa tried the word out and decided she liked it. "Thank you," she said.

Elsdon looked startled, but Nyssa was willing to take any compliment she could get.

"And you're . . ." Nyssa said, wanting to return the favor, ". . . surprising."

"Surprising," Elsdon repeated.

"In a good way," she assured him.

He must not be used to compliments, either, for she thought he looked embarrassed and pleased. He lay back down on his blanket.

"Think about what you saw the day my parents died," Nyssa advised. "I think that will help."

Elsdon closed his eyes.

So did Nyssa.

This time Elsdon is fifteen years old.

He is running, but this is no rancid-tasting fear dream. The alternating heat and coolness on his face as he runs first in the sunlight between buildings, then in the shade they throw off, the prickle of sweat on his scalp that works its way down the sides of his face, the foul smell as he jumps over where someone has emptied a chamber pot in the alley—these details are too vivid to be anything but true memory.

No one is chasing Elsdon. He is running TO something, not AWAY. But Nyssa can't tell what it is because he is spending all his thoughts on getting there as quickly as possible—"Don't let me be too late" is the only phrase she can glean from his jumbled thoughts, that and more basic single-word commands to the straining muscles of his legs: "Left." "Jump." "Faster."

She knows he has had a vision of impending doom for someone, but Elsdon is not thinking of the vision, just that he needs to keep it from coming true. He has had other, vaguer visions of this coming violence, but he has not known enough to do more than make people suspicious. But now he feels this is the day.

Then Nyssa becomes aware of another stink, one she's all too familiar with: rotting flesh and tannin baths. She knows, a moment before Elsdon does, that he's approaching Tanners' Alley. She feels his elation as he realizes he's almost there. She realizes that she recognizes the shops and buildings, and she knows exactly the shortcut he's taking as he breaks through to Woodworkers' Street, dashes across the street, and bangs on the closed door of her own father's shop.

From next door, a dog starts barking.

"Let me in!" Elsdon demands, loudly enough for someone entering a shop three doors down to pause and glance back to see what is happening.

There is no answer from inside the shop.

Elsdon jiggles the latch, but the door is locked for the evening. He places his ear against the wood of the door and from inside can hear raised voices.

Nyssa realizes she's overhearing her parents being murdered.

Through Elsdon's memory Nyssa can hear her mother's words. "You're a beast," Mother is shouting, "a cruel, selfish beast."

But it is not some unknown intruder who responds. Nyssa hears her own father's voice shout back: "You're a breeder of witches. You're a witch yourself, for all I know. How do I even know she's mine?"

Nyssa feels the pain in the side of Elsdon's fist, a pain he's not even aware of himself as he beats against the door.

Something hits the door with a thud, something thrown. Nyssa, from her own memory of the room and how it looked after the bodies were found, knows it is a candlestick.

Elsdon realizes that no one is going to open the door and that he is certainly not going to be able to beat it down. Distracted, thinking that he IS too late after all, he steps back from the door for a better look at the house itself. He sees a window on the side between this shop and the next.

He runs to the side of the house. The window is high up off the ground, just above eye level, for it is meant to let light inside and to allow the occupants to look out, not to encourage outsiders to look in. But Elsdon grabs hold of the sill and jumps, swinging his right leg up while he braces his left foot against the wall. He scrambles to re-adjust his handholds and gets his left knee up onto the sill next to his right foot. He is crouched in the window.

From the neighbor's window behind him, the dog is barking in a frenzy. But Elsdon pays no attention to that. He is swinging his left leg up from under him, shifting his balance, about to leap into the room. There are only two people in the room, the woodworker he has been having visions of all this past week and the man's wife.

Nyssa, of course, recognizes her parents.

The man has hold of the woman by the shoulders, and he is shaking her.

"Stop!" Elsdon commands.

Neither of the room's other two occupants seems aware of him.

"You will NOT send her away," the woman screams.

"I will send you both away," the man counters. "I will denounce you both as witches. You bewitched me to marry you, and that makes our marriage null and your offspring bastards."

The woman screams, an angry, wordless scream, and she spits in his face.

He hurls her back violently, and she trips over the candlestick one of them had thrown earlier. She falls, striking her head against the wall, and the shelf above her jostles loose, showering her with the most delicate of the

woodcarver's works—the ones with pieces of rare and expensive glass and mirror, which he has put out of the way especially because they are so fragile. In a rage the man picks up a chisel, sharp enough to gouge wood, and buries it in the woman's chest.

Elsdon, who has just leaped off the window sill and into the room, and Nyssa, tied to his vision, watch in helpless horror. The woman is probably already dead before the clatter of falling, settling objects ceases.

The only sound is the barking of the dog.

The woodworker looks as shocked as Elsdon feels. The man takes a step forward, but then two steps back. He looks around the room as if seeking help, seeking a way out of this situation, and he spies Elsdon. His eyes flicker from his dead wife to the youth who has just climbed through his window. And now he is no longer hesitant. He steps purposefully toward Elsdon, delayed only because he has to circle around the wood-sawing frame, and then for another moment as he picks up a piece of board.

Elsdon knows what everyone will think if he's found in here. He knows what the woodworker can claim: that he heard someone climbing through the window, heard his wife scream, and walked in just in time to see Elsdon kill his poor wife. For there is no excuse Elsdon can give for being here—no excuse that people won't find more vile than th thought that he's a murderer. No one will fault this man f killing his wife's killer. All that, IF Elsdon is found in he

In a moment, Elsdon leaps back up onto the sill. finds himself face-to-face with the barking dog of the n bor across the alley. But that neighbor's window is too for the dog to get through, much as the dog looks as

that's its intent. Elsdon jumps down into the alley and out between the two buildings. He is running in the street once more, this time thinking, "Too late. Too late again."

Nyssa sat up, shivering. "That's not true," she protested, furious that her voice was shaking, that she sounded close to tears. "My father did not kill my mother."

Elsdon knew enough not to come close, not to try to comfort her. "You should know," he said, "whether these true-memory dreams of yours can lie."

She hated him almost as much as she had before, because she knew they could not.

"I'm sorry," he said.

This was why Elsdon had refused to tell her. He knew she wouldn't believe him.

"It doesn't make sense," she protested. "He was killed, too." For a few moments during the dream, she had thought she would see Elsdon kill her father, and she knew—after what she'd just seen—that she wouldn't have blamed him for it, that she wouldn't even have hated him for it.

But there had been no time. She knew from Thurmond's dream that there hadn't been time between Mother's scream and Elsdon's running. No time for Elsdon to kill her father. No time—or reason—to wait around for Worrell to come in and then strike him down also.

"What about the rest of it?" Nyssa protested.

Elsdon stood up. He opened the door to let in

light and air, and leaned against the door frame, drained after all the sensations of the two true-memory dreams. It was still only midafternoon.

Nyssa flung away the dagger that had brought Elsdon's memories for her to see. "You're wrong," she told him, knowing what he suspected—for there was no other explanation, and she suspected it herself.

"There could have been another intruder," Elsdon told her. "Someone who came in through a different window."

Nyssa tried to clutch that thought to her, but she wasn't that witless. She knew it was unlikely.

"We'll never know for sure," Elsdon said, "for you've run out of witnesses. And maybe that's for the best."

Yes, Nyssa thought.

She wanted to leave it at that. She told herself to leave it at that.

"No," Nyssa said. "No, there was another witness."

Part of herself tried to warn her away, but she ran her hands up and down over her skirt. She flicked away a crusty bit of something that came loose, probably some dried bit of the stew she'd been helping Maddy prepare for dinner. There was dirt and a twig she'd picked up from the floor of the blind, and she ignored that. What was left were three short, hairlike strands: Rufus's fur.

"Nyssa." Elsdon shook his head.

She clutched the fur in her dirty hand and laid

her head back down. There was no telling if this would work. Did animals dream as people did? Did they have memories? The one thing she did know was that dogs seemed to take a lot of naps, so she probably wouldn't have to wait long before Rufus fell asleep.

She herself felt drained from all she was experiencing and quietly fell asleep yet again.

First came the gentle ripples of a wish dream, Rufus chasing down a rat. . . .

After a good chase, in which the rat is clever but Rufus is cleverer, and the rat is fast but Rufus is faster, and the rat is strong but Rufus is stronger—after all that, Rufus snaps the rat's neck. He brings the creature to his master, setting it down at his feet.

Master, sitting in his chair, leans down, much more movement than Master really can do anymore. He pats Rufus on the head, scratches under his chin, speaks in a strong and clear voice, though Rufus doesn't recognize any of the words but his own name and "Good dog." Rufus pants happily.

Surely, Nyssa worried, a dog who had lived seven years and had its own needs and cravings and interests—such as they were—couldn't be expected to be thinking about what she needed him to be thinking about.

Rufus didn't see in color, but as another dream began, Nyssa recognized the wealth of smells and sounds she'd never experienced before as the details of true memory.

Perhaps it came from seeing Nyssa two days in a row after not seeing her for so long, or maybe from seeing Elsdon and associating him with the violent events of six years before. Or maybe, she thought, her own desires *did* affect which memories came forth in dreams.

Whatever the reason, Rufus remembered his own version of that day. . . .

Master and young-master-who-sometimes-kicks-and-teases-when-Master-isn't-looking are arguing—Rufus doesn't understand the words, but he does understand the angry tones. Rufus does not like angry tones, associating them with the man-who-owned-She-Who-Gave-Milk-and-sold-Rufus-to-Master.

Rufus barks to show he does not like the angry words, but nobody listens.

Rufus is happy when young-master-who-sometimes-kicks-and-teases-when-Master-isn't-looking leaves.

Rufus barks to show he is happy and to tell young-master-who-sometimes-kicks-and-teases-when-Master-isn't-looking not to come back.

Master works wood for a man-who-stands-outside, which makes Master happy, which makes Rufus happier yet.

Master gives the pieces of wood to the man-who-stands-outside, who then goes away.

Master starts putting things in those places that means Master is about to stop working on wood and start making food, which makes Rufus even happier than his usual being happy when Master is happy.

But before Master is finished, Rufus hears something outside. Rufus has been hearing a lot of things, but this is more interesting. Rufus runs to the door and sees a boy-pounding-on-the-door-next-door. The boy-pounding-on-the-door-next-door is shouting something, but the words are not "Rufus" or "Good dog" or "Food," so Rufus doesn't know what he's saying. Though the boy-pounding-on-the-door-next-door sounds angry, Rufus thinks he smells frightened.

Rufus barks in case there's something-to-be-frightened-of that needs to be warned away from Master's house.

The boy-pounding-on-the-door-next-door runs to the side of the house, and Rufus runs to the window to keep on watching him.

The boy-pounding-on-the-door-next-door has become the boy-climbing-into-the-window-next-door. Climbing into windows is something Rufus understands people are not supposed to do, so he barks to let the boy know he should stop.

The boy ignores Rufus. Over his shoulder, Rufus sees both the man-who-lives-next-door and the woman-who-lives-next-door. They are shouting at each other, angry.

Rufus barks to let them know they should stop.

"Rufus!" Master commands.

Rufus barks to tell Master that he should come to the window, too, to see.

The woman-who-lives-next-door screams, and the man-who-lives-next-door pushes her so that she falls, and things fall on her, and Rufus can smell blood.

Rufus barks: danger, danger, danger.

The boy-climbing-into-the-window-next-door climbs out of the window, jumps to the ground, and then runs away. Master finally goes to the door and yells something after him.

Then Master sternly commands, "Rufus!"

Rufus returns to the window and sees the boy-who-lives-next-door run into the room. The boy-who-lives-next-door runs to the bloody woman-who-lives-next-door and starts yelling at the man-who-lives-next-door.

Rufus barks to let them know yelling is bad, but they don't listen. The boy and the man are shoving each other, and the man hits the boy on the head with a piece of wood. Rufus smells more blood. The boy picks something up and brings it down very heavily onto the man's head. Even more blood.

Master puts away the last of the wood and says to Rufus, "Let's eat, Rufus-boy."

Rufus knows "eat" is another word for food. He tries to tell Master that something dangerous happened next door, but Master is walking to the food room, and Rufus doesn't know what to do. Rufus decides that if something-dangerous comes into Master's house, Rufus will bite it until it goes away. But for now Rufus follows Master toward the food.

Twelve

The door to the hunting blind was still open, though Elsdon was neither in the room nor in the doorway.

Nyssa realized she didn't know what she felt.

Angry, she decided. Above all the other emotions, mostly she was angry.

She rubbed her hands clean onto her skirt.

You knew you shouldn't look, she told herself. *Even Elsdon tried to warn you.*

Witless girl.

She thought she had her expression composed when she stepped outside and found Elsdon sitting on the bench, but one look at his face told her that she must have looked about to fall over. He started to scramble to his feet, and she commanded, "Stay," as though she were talking to Rufus.

She walked past him, though her sense of direction was confused, and she was not sure if she was heading back toward town or farther into the woods. When she tried to work out which she wanted, she realized she didn't know, so she got off the path and walked among the trees instead.

Faster and faster she walked, not sure why, except maybe to outdistance her thoughts.

If that was what she wanted, she thought, she obviously wasn't going fast enough. She began to run, though branches snagged at her hair and clothing, scratched her arms, tripped her. Over and over she picked herself up and ran some more, frightening herself, frightening the wildlife about her. And still her thoughts were able to keep pace with her.

She slipped on a pile of last year's leaves and slid headlong down a short embankment, finding herself near the edge of a creek, with one arm soaked up to the elbow and her knees scraped and bruised.

And there was Worrell, walking along the bank, dressed in the gray habit of a monk, with the crown of his head shaved. He had his hands clasped behind his back, and he was looking perfectly calm, as though meditating on some important though not personally involving aspect of spirituality.

"You'd better join a monastery," she shouted at him.

"Hello, Nyssa," Worrell responded gently.

She ran up to him and began beating him on the chest.

He didn't fight her off but waited until, finally exhausted, she leaned into him and began to cry. Then he waited for the tears to stop. Then he tipped her chin up so that she had to look at him. "Are you crying because I killed Father?" he asked.

She shook her head. After seeing Elsdon's memory, she had known she'd be willing to forgive Elsdon if he'd done it, so why not her own brother? "He was a bully who had just killed Mother, who would have blamed someone else for it, and who was attacking you. He may well have ended up trying to convince people you had done it. If I could have everything back the way it was, with both him and Mother alive, I would. But, no, I'm not crying because he's dead, and I'm not crying because you killed him."

"Why, then?" Worrell asked. "Because you feel justice demands you tell people what you learned, but you can't without revealing how you know?"

"No," Nyssa said. "I don't feel the need to tell anyone. Justice . . ." she sighed, realizing the truth of what she was about to say, ". . . justice has been served."

She sat down on the bank of the creek, and Worrell sat down next to her, his arm companionably around her shoulders. He smelled faintly, she thought, of incense.

She asked, "Why didn't you tell me? Did you not remember? Because of the blow to your head?"

Worrell hesitated as though he might be considering agreeing with her. "I was dazed," he finally said. "Not only by being smacked by that length of wood, but by seeing what he'd done to Mother and by realizing what I'd done to him. I was sitting there, watching the room get dark, wishing it would all go away, half thinking that if night came and obscured everything, when it got light again, I would find everything as it had been." He sighed. "Then you came in. Talking of intruders. And, oh, Nyssa, my head hurt, and each time the vein in my head pulsed, I could taste my own blood, and I knew I was going to die, and it was just easier not to tell you, and to let you go."

"I didn't know how badly hurt you were," Nyssa told him. "I would have stayed."

"It wouldn't have made any difference," Worrell told her.

"You wouldn't have been alone." Nyssa thought of Elsdon's brother Severin, and how he'd been surrounded by father, brother, and three stablehands, and still had died alone. "You could have been so much," she said, thinking of him as master woodcrafter, or town guard, or father, or monk.

She felt his hand against her cheek, as solid, as real as a true-memory dream. "Don't be crazy anymore," he said.

"I'll try," she promised. "Elsdon says I'm not crazy, just persistent."

Worrell gave his engaging grin. "Elsdon may well know more than any truly sane man should about crazy and not-crazy and sometimes-crazy and used-to-be-crazy."

From behind, Nyssa heard a twig break, then Elsdon came sliding down the bank, holding a branch to keep from coming down headfirst the way she had.

Even the small amount of sleep Elsdon had finally gotten seemed to have taken some of the edge off him—that, or knowing she now knew what had happened. Fidgety nerves had softened to obvious but simple exhaustion.

He looked at her warily. "Are you all right?" he asked.

Not warily, she realized, *concerned.*

She nodded.

Elsdon hesitated. "I thought I heard you talking to someone."

"To my brother," Nyssa said.

"Ah," Elsdon said, maybe edging now a little bit back toward that wariness. "The one who died."

"I know he's dead," she said. Well, usually she did. "But he was a good brother. Sometimes it helps for me to picture him, to imagine what he'd say. Sometimes . . . sometimes I convince myself that he is still here, helping me." She began to cry once more. "My father always said I was witless."

Elsdon knelt beside her, where—a moment before—Worrell had seemed to be. "Your father called anyone who disagreed with him witless. You're steadfast and brave and honest, and you did the best you could with what you were given."

She looked up at him, startled.

"The only witless thing I've ever seen you do is

believe your father." He put his arms around her and let her cry, and when she was finished picked the leaves and debris out of her hair.

All this while, she thought, she'd been accusing him of something he hadn't done, of something he had tried with all his might to prevent.

"I'm sorry," Elsdon said again. "I wish . . ." He sighed and shook his head, because—obviously—one wish was not enough to fix either of their lives. "Come with me," he said. "To Sterling. No one knows either one of us. We can pretend to be whatever we want to be."

"You and me?" she asked. "Together?" Then, because her mother had raised her to be a good girl, "What, exactly, are you asking us to pretend to be?"

Elsdon blushed, which Nyssa found becoming. "I'm asking us to *pretend to be* normal. I'm asking us to *actually be* friends—the kind of friends who watch out for each other and who are there to talk to when times get rough, but also when times are good. I'm certainly hoping for more good times than rough ones. I'd like us to be the kind of friends who might, eventually, decide together that they want to be more than friends."

He was a lord's son; she was a woodcrafter's daughter. Their class difference would be a huge obstacle. And two witches together would doubtless find it harder to hide their natures than either one alone. And yet . . . And yet each of them had been alone for so long.

Nyssa hated making decisions, because a girl who had spent so much of her life thinking of herself as witless could get herself into all sorts of trouble with wrong choices.

But the reasons to say yes tugged at her much more strongly than the reasons to say no.

So she said, “Yes.”